MW01123735

Faeries of Saizia

for Shaylan

Enjoy '13

Tonya L Chaves

TONYA L. CHAVES

Copyright © 2018 Tonya L. Chaves.

All rights reserved. No part of this book may be reproduced, stored, or transmitted by any means—whether auditory, graphic, mechanical, or electronic—without written permission of the author, except in the case of brief excerpts used in critical articles and reviews. Unauthorized reproduction of any part of this work is illegal and is punishable by law.

This is a work of fiction. All of the characters, names, incidents, organizations, and dialogue in this novel are either the products of the author's imagination or are used fictitiously.

ISBN: 978-1-4834-9070-0 (sc)
ISBN: 978-1-4834-9069-4 (e)

Library of Congress Control Number: 2018911253

Because of the dynamic nature of the Internet, any web addresses or links contained in this book may have changed since publication and may no longer be valid. The views expressed in this work are solely those of the author and do not necessarily reflect the views of the publisher, and the publisher hereby disclaims any responsibility for them.

Any people depicted in stock imagery provided by Getty Images are models, and such images are being used for illustrative purposes only. Certain stock imagery © Getty Images.

Interior Image Credit: Tonya L. Chaves

Lulu Publishing Services rev. date: 10/4/2018

To my beautiful children,
who inspire my imagination daily

CONTENTS

ACKNOWLEDGMENTS

This was a work in progress for so long that my list of those who helped along the way may be too long to mention, but I will try.

First and foremost, thanks to Lulu Press for walking me through this process like a helpless toddler.

Thanks also to my children—Daniel, Molly, and Ruby—for giving me the inspiration to create my own bedtime stories.

My parents and family encouraged me by always telling me that I can do and be anything I set my mind to.

A big shout out to all my *The Bloggess* pals, especially Bjørn Larssen, for all the valuable creative criticism and insight I so desperately needed. You all are always in my pocket. KKMF!

Darren Brown, thank you for all your publishing advice and encouragement.

Thank you to those I have loved and lost in this world. In memory of Teresa Gail Chaves and Richard Brian Snow, both of whom would be very proud to see this book has come to fruition. I miss you both.

CE

CHAPTER 1

Celebration

Avery sat on the edge of his disheveled bed, wiping the sleep from his tired eyes. He wildly ran his hands through his short, messy brown hair. He had a big day ahead of him and needed to start getting dressed. He stood up, yawned, and stretched out his iridescent silvery wings.

Not only was it the first day of summer—and a hot one at that—but it was his birthday, a very important day for a faerie. Today Avery turned one hundred years old, which in human years was the equivalent of a teenager. When a faerie turned one hundred, he or she was given an important responsibility in the forest, but no one knew what that responsibility was until the high queen, Yamani, announced it on the faerie's birthday night. Even Yamani would not know until just before then, when Avery would tell the flowers his name, and they would whisper his destiny to Yamani.

It was so hot that Avery's wings felt like they were about to melt, and he still had to put on his festivities garb. He looked with disdain at his snakeskin jerkin lying next to him, sighed, and then carefully slid it over his wings and pulled his arms through. He caught a glimpse of himself in the mirror and thought he looked ridiculous.

He was struggling with the stiff clasp on his belt when he heard his best friend, Zäria calling to him from outside.

"Avery, what is taking you so long? They've already started the music and dance. I want to go too. Hurry!" She had turned one hundred two months earlier. The high queen's flowers had given her the duty of tending to the royal gardens. Avery felt the queen was always easy on Zäria, perhaps because Zäria was an orphan.

Avery splashed a little water on his wings and arranged the down feathers the best he could. While walking to the door, he shouted to Zäria, "I'm almost ready. It's just so hot my wings keep drooping." He opened the door and stepped a boot-clad foot outside.

"Hey, not bad," Zäria said as she giggled at him. "Are you sure you want to wear your feathers like that?"

"Yes, let's just go. I'm melting in this stuff." He closed the door and waited for Zäria to stop fussing with his clothes. He noticed that there was something different about her but couldn't figure it out. Her hair was as long and yellow as it was yesterday. Maybe she was wearing new flowers in her hair. He just shrugged and ushered her down the dirt path.

Black and gray river rock, lush green shrubbery, and wild flowers lined the short path from Avery's house to the palace. The smell of wild jasmine tickled his nose. When Avery and Zäria arrived, they found the rest of the forest faeries already had started celebrating.

Avery noticed each faerie was dressed in his or her best with circlets of flowers in their hair. He suddenly felt even more self-conscious in his absurd garb. He watched the group of faeries as they danced, their iridescent wings and dress creating a rainbow of colors.

He looked over to the palace and saw that Yamani had already been announced and was sitting on her throne of acorns and oak leaves, dressed in a red rose-petal gown. Avery saw several young faeries sitting on handmade quilts in the mossy grass at the foot of the palace steps. He remembered doing the same when he was younger. He would much rather be watching from the courtyard than being the center of attention today.

Avery thought about running back home when the royal adviser stood up and shouted, "Hear ye! Hear ye! May I have your utmost attention?" Everyone stopped what they were doing, and Avery knew he had missed his chance to run.

"It is now time to commence with the Ceremony of Duty," the royal adviser announced. "We are honoring the one hundredth birthday of Avery Lightfoot. He will now come forward and speak his name to the high queen's flowers."

Avery glanced at Zäria, who winked at him. He blushed as he made his way to the throne. He bowed to the high queen and stepped up to where her flowers were growing in the stones next to her. The flowers were believed to hold special magic since they grew in a place where they shouldn't be able to survive. Other than that, Avery thought they looked like ordinary gardenias. The flowers gave off the sweetest, most fragrant smell as Avery crouched down to them. He took one last whiff of their sweet fragrance and spoke clearly. "Vital Flowers of the high queen Yamani, I have come to receive my responsibility to the forest of Saizia. My name is Avery Lightfoot, and I am one hundred today."

Avery bowed to the flowers and then to Yamani. She nodded to him in return, and then he backed off the steps to wait for his orders.

The high queen rose from her throne and sat down on a small stone next to the flowers. She gave them a drink of water and then whispered to them.

Avery held his breath, trying to hear the queen or the flowers, but he heard nothing. He wondered if the flowers whispered at all or if this whole ceremony was just a waste of time.

Avery watched as Yamani leaned in close to her garden, thanked the flowers, and returned to take her place on the throne. Avery thought the queen's voice was both beautiful and powerful as she spoke.

"Faeries of Saizia, today is an important day for us—the first day of summer, when we must all strive to care for the forest beings. For Avery, who has turned one hundred today and will take on his responsibility to the forest, the Vital Flowers have made their decision and have confided it to me. Avery, step forward."

Avery nervously approached Yamani, bowed his head, and waited.

Yamani said, "Avery Lightfoot, your duty to the forest, as of your one hundredth year of being, is to care for and protect the toadstools."

Avery reflexively smirked and then quickly gave his practiced response. "Thank you, High Queen Yamani, and thank you, Vital Flowers. I shall take on my duties in Saizia with pride and respect." He bowed to Yamani and turned to the crowd of faeries.

Cheers and applause broke out, and Avery bashfully smiled at them. He stepped down into the crowd and accepted some handshakes and congratulations. He found Zäria in the crowd and nudged her away from everyone.

"So, Master of the Toadstools, what will be your first death-defying task?" Zäria said as she giggled.

"Very funny, Zäria," responded Avery. "I'm actually relieved that my duty is to the toadstools. How hard could that be, really?"

"Well, you never know. They might just start growing out of hand, and the whole forest could turn into one giant fungus." She laughed so hard that tears flowed from her eyes.

Avery thought about it and laughed along with her. "I guess that would be a funny sight," he said. "Come on, Zäria. I want to get out of this garb and fly over to the pond." He tugged Zäria by her arm.

"Hey, I don't want to watch you undress, you crazy winged creature," Zäria joked.

"Good. I was planning on gluing your eyes shut anyway. Let's go before the elders wanna give me advice on the best ways to care for toadstools."

When they reached Avery's house, a passing ladybug stopped to chat. Avery quietly slipped away into the house to change, leaving Zäria with the chatty ladybug. Zäria had always been good with all the insects in the forest, which was a trait Avery wished he had. He seemed to accidentally insult them every time he opened his mouth. Like the time he called a pill bug a roly-poly, which was very offensive to it. Maybe that was why he and Zäria were such good friends. She did all the talking, and at times he felt she could almost read his mind.

Once Avery had changed, he poked his head out the door to see if Zäria was ready to go.

"Leapin' lizards! You nearly scared the wings off me, Avery!" Zäria blurted as she jumped back.

"Oh, sorry. I didn't realize you were right by the door. Are you ready to head out?"

"I suppose," she said. She tousled her hair while trying to get it back in place, although Avery didn't see anything wrong with it. "Why do you want to go to the pond? We go there all the time. Can't we go somewhere else? Somewhere we've never been?"

"Like where?" Avery asked.

"I don't know. I've never been there, silly." Zäria left her hair alone and rolled her eyes at him. She took flight and spun around over Avery's head.

Avery called to her, "I want to talk to King Toad and let him know that I will be caring for all the toadstools. I think he will be helpful." He saw the disappointed look on Zäria's face and added, "Then I suppose we could go explore somewhere new in the forest. Maybe the king will have some suggestions. I hear he has gone on many trips to the edge of the forest."

"Okay, but if those tadpoles of his pull any tricks this time, I'm never going to the pond with you again."

"Deal," he laughed. Zäria smiled back at him. He liked it when she smiled; her bright-green eyes sparkled in the sunlight when she was happy.

"I don't know how you can get along with all the flying insects in the forest but none of the water life," Avery observed

Zäria flew past him. "I guess it's just easier for me to get along with creatures I have something in common with. You know I can't swim. Those rude tadpoles keep trying to get me into the pond."

Avery laughed softly. He could tell she was getting angry just talking about being near the water. He didn't blame her. He recalled the time when Zäria had fallen into the pond while she was learning to fly. Queen Yamani had sent her guards to fish her out, and the royal sorceress had to revive her. He had wondered how the queen knew Zäria was in trouble but was grateful that she had acted fast to save his best friend.

"I'll make sure the tadpoles leave you alone," Avery said, trying to sound protective. He hooked his arm under Zäria's elbow as they both took flight. As the pond came into view, Avery admired its beauty. Light trickled down through the tree leaves and danced on the calm blue water, making it glisten. It reminded him of Zäria's eyes.

Avery and Zäria flew over to the palace to speak to the king on Ribbit Rock. The toad king's palace was inside a big tree in the middle of the pond. They landed on a branch, and Avery called down to the crickets guarding the door. "Hello."

"Who goes there?" one of the crickets asked, looking around for where the voice had come from.

Avery called down again. "We are up here, in the branches." They slowly let themselves down to speak to the crickets. "Sorry. We didn't want to frighten you by plopping right in front of you without warning."

"Much obliged, but you already scared the wings off us," the first cricket said.

"What business do you two have at Ribbit Rock?" the second asked. He didn't strike Avery as having much of a personality.

"My name is Zäria, and this is my friend Avery," she began. "We would like to speak to King Hubert if we may."

The less-friendly cricket replied, "The king is very busy at this time of year. There are lots of tadpoles to tend to."

"It will only take a few minutes. I am the newest caretaker of the toadstools," Avery said. "I just wanted to introduce myself and see if the king has any suggestions or instructions on how he would like me to tend to them."

One cricket nodded to the other, who disappeared into the palace and returned a moment later. He said, "The king will see you both now. Please come in, and mind your manners. King Hubert does not take kindly to insolence."

Of the many times Avery had visited the pond, this was the first time he had been inside the king's palace. It wasn't anything like Yamani's palace. There weren't any flowers at all. Yamani kept flowers everywhere. The toad's palace was extremely green. Moss grew along the inside walls of the tree. It was also very wet and made

Avery's wings feel sticky. He looked at Zäria and noticed that her smile had faded and fear seemed to be in its place. He instinctively clasped her hand and pulled her a bit closer to him.

"Avery, we're not going to fall into the pond from in here are we?" Zäria said as she squeezed Avery's hand a bit tighter.

"I told you I'd watch out for you. It's all right," Avery assured her.

When they arrived at the king's throne, they both bowed to the large green toad.

The king spoke first. "What brings faeries to my palace?" He smirked at them, seeming amused by the visit.

"I'm Avery Lightfoot. As I'm sure Your Highness is aware, the faeries are given a duty to the forest on their one hundredth birthday, Avery continued on. "I was given the responsibility of caring for and protecting the toadstools. Thought you might have suggestions on how to tend to them, Your Highness."

The king stared at them for a moment, as if he was contemplating this idea. "No faerie has every come to me and asked for my advice on how anything should be cared for in my kingdom. Why have you decided to come to me today, young faerie?"

Avery was a little surprised by this comment. "Your Highness, it only made sense to me that you would have some say in the matter of the care and protection of the toadstools. I know they are important in your kingdom, and you should be involved in the matter of their care, I believe ... uh, Your Highness," he sputtered.

"That is a most wise and appreciated consideration. I've always thought the faeries were a self-indulgent species. You seem to have proven my suspicions wrong. In my opinion, the toadstools take care of themselves for the most part, but it would be nice if they were given some attention. Perhaps you should seek advice from the current toadstool caretakers. I'm sorry I could not be more helpful." The king fiddled with the many trinkets hanging from his throne. He signaled for his guards to come forward. "Please escort our faerie friends back to their side of the pond." King Hubert turned back to Avery and Zäria. "This was a most interesting and pleasant visit. I hope we meet again."

"It was our pleasure to meet with you today. I will heed your advice and speak with the faeries of the toadstool regime. Good day to you."

"Good day, Your Highness," Zäria echoed.

They bowed and turned to follow their escorts to the edge of the pond, where they took flight and waved back at the guards.

CHAPTER 2

Adventure

"Where do you want to go now Zäria?" Avery asked. "I know you've been dying for your 'adventure' and all." He chuckled a bit under his breath.

"It's not funny, Avery," Zäria said with a huff. "Don't you ever just want to see something new? Something different? I mean, we're one hundred years old and have no stories to tell of it. I don't want to tell my grandchildren that all I ever did was take care of flowers in the queen's garden and collect seeds."

"You are being a little overly dramatic. What about the splinter of '82?"

"Getting a splinter yanked from my behind is not something I wish to discuss with anyone, and I wish you would stop bringing it up."

He grinned at Zäria. "Well, in that case, sliding down tree branches is out of the question."

"Avery Lightfoot, you are completely hopeless." Zäria crossed her arms, turning away from him.

Avery thought for a moment, his expression becoming more solemn. He turned away from Zäria and walked a few paces, and then, as if finally deciding to speak, he said, "Fine. Let's go to Eerie Hollow."

Zäria's mouth dropped open, and she steadied herself on a dandelion leaf. "Eerie Hollow? Are you crazy? We can't go there. It's haunted. Have you forgotten that Millie hasn't spoken a word to anyone since she stumbled out of there fifty years ago?"

"Exactly. That was fifty years ago. That 'ghost' should be bored with Eerie Hollow by now. Besides, we don't know what happened to her because, as you said, she hasn't spoken. Maybe she took a vow of silence, or just lost her voice, or she just doesn't have anything to say."

Zäria looked at Avery as if he had lost his mind. "I'm sure none of those reasons are correct. Lost her voice for fifty years? Really? Well, I did want an adventure. What better place than Eerie Hollow, where no faerie has been in half a century? Let's go."

Avery didn't expect her to agree to this half-brained idea. Before he could say anything about it, Zäria started on a rant. She flitted around like a crazed hummingbird, picking at plants and flowers, talking all the while. "Should we wait till dark? What should we take with us? Some fireflies, for certain, and maybe some seeds and berry juice. I wonder what would scare a ghost away if we were to come face-to-face—or rather, face-to-apparition. We have to protect ourselves, don't we?"

Zäria was talking so fast that Avery had a tough time keeping up with her. He didn't have a chance to answer a single question before she asked another. After becoming slightly dizzy from trying to follow her, he finally blurted out, "Zäria! Zäria! You have to calm down a bit."

She stopped in midair, stopped flapping her wings, and floated back to the toadstool she had abandoned moments ago.

"If we are going there," Avery said, "we can't tell anyone. We will have to go tonight since we both have to return to our duties in the morning."

Zäria nodded in agreement. "Right. Tonight, we go."

"What are we waiting for? Let's go now." Avery grasped Zäria's hand and took flight.

Zäria shouted, "Wait! Don't we need supplies? Fireflies, food, anything?"

"Nope. I said we can't tell anyone. That includes fireflies. And I'm sure there are nuts and seeds in Eerie Hollow. Heck, they might even be better than anything we've ever had."

Zäria stopped at a patch of boysenberry bushes at the end of the dell, where she absentmindedly picked berries and tossed them in her satchel. When Avery reached for her hand, Zäria snapped out of her daze. He had never held her hand before. She suddenly forgot how scared she was. As long as Avery was holding her hand, she felt safe.

Still hand in hand, they flew over the boysenberry bushes, past the last patch of dandelions, and straight into Eerie Hollow. Zäria held her breath, but nothing happened. They didn't see any ghosts, the weather didn't change, and they didn't fall into an alternate dimension.

Remembering Millie, Zäria said, "Avery?"

"Yes?"

"Nothing. Just wanted to be sure I didn't become mute like Millie."

"We haven't even seen the ghost yet."

She shuddered. "Don't remind me. I don't want to meet with any spirits or apparitions."

"Oh, Zäria, where's your sense of adventure?"

Zäria merely rolled her eyes.

The wind whistled through the nearby bushes and rustled the leaves, causing Zäria to nearly jump out of her wings. Avery laughed nervously, but that only upset her more.

"You'll only draw attention to us if you jump every time the leaves move," Avery said.

"I can't help it. We shouldn't be here"

"You want to leave? We can go back to Saizia, but I thought you wanted to go on an adventure."

Zäria looked back across the field. She could faintly hear the music and carrying-on of the other faeries during the festivities of the day. She shrugged her shoulders and straightened out her wings. "I didn't say I wanted to leave," she said defensively. "I'm fine. Let's stay. I want to look around. Maybe we'll find out what really happened to Millie."

Among the tall trees, it was a bit darker and colder, making Zäria's wings flutter to keep warm. This did nothing for her nerves. They pressed on anyway, carefully observing everything. Zäria wondered what lurked in the shadows. What had scared Millie? What would they find in this forbidden world?

After a few moments of flying in silence, Avery started humming. Zäria looked at him and grinned at the silly childhood song. Avery stopped singing to say, "You know, this isn't too bad, actually. No one bossing you around, annoying you with boring stories. Just flying in the peaceful darkness, breathing in the fresh, chocolate-scented air—"

"Chocolate-scented air?" Zäria said and took a deep breath. "You're right; it does smell like chocolate."

"Wonder why it would smell like chocolate this far into the hollow."

The two flew farther into the hollow, following the delicious scent. As the scent grew stronger, Zäria also detected other scrumptiously sweet aromas, like toasted marshmallows, caramel, and peppermint. The aroma enveloped them while they flew in closer. Zäria saw a light up ahead and faintly heard voices in the distance.

Zäria and Avery quietly hid behind a couple of trees and peered over some overgrown bushes at their base. Zäria was amazed and surprised at what she saw. Three figures, just a few trees ahead of them, were gathered around a fire with a pot larger than them. Zäria noticed they were slightly smaller than faeries, but similar in appearance, except they lacked wings.

"I think they're elves, but I've never seen any before," whispered Zäria.

"I wonder what they're doing here. They must be keeping their presence secret, or Yamani would have invited them to our village for the celebrations," said Avery.

"Do you think they're friendly? I really would like to have some of those delicious-smelling sweets they are making," Zäria said dreamily.

"I think we should stay hidden for now, at least until we have observed them for a while. We don't know if they are who Millie ran into. And it seems like something is not right about them being here."

Avery and Zäria stayed behind the trees and bushes while they watched the elves busily prepare all the chocolate confections. The three elves were moving peppermints and chocolate from a storage hold to each of the pots over the fire. The one pushing the cart was a portly fellow with a bright-red nose and spiky brown hair. He sort of wobbled when he walked, and Zäria had to hold in her laughter. The other two were much smaller and wiry. They also looked a bit younger and so similar in appearance that she thought they might be twins.

Zäria listened carefully to the elves' conversation.

"You two quit getting in the way, and keep these peppermints in the cart. We don't want them covered in dirt," said the portly elf.

"Ah, Gus, why not?" said one of the twins. "Dirt-covered peppermint is the only flavor we haven't made yet." He chuckled.

"Yeah, we could even throw in some beetles and rocks for added flavor and crunchiness," the other twin chimed in.

The portly elf they called Gus gave them a sideward glance. "Very funny, but I don't think Thordon would find it quite the barrel of laughs you two have found it. Sprout, throw a couple more peppermints into that pot of chocolate, and Bean, you take the rest back to Grimm's. I'm going to check to see if the fire needs more wood."

Bean quickly asked, "Check the fire, or check on Veena?"

Gus threw Bean a warning glance and walked off.

"What?" Bean asked Sprout. "I was only joking."

"Just do what he said, Bean. You know that Thordon has been really hard on Gus since that faerie found us."

"Yeah, I heard that 'Wings' won't be talking any time soon either." Bean laughed.

Zäria and Avery looked at each other and whispered "Millie" at the same time. They waited for the elves to walk out of view and then quietly turned around and made their way out of Eerie Hollow. Neither one breathed a word until they were safe in Saizia again.

Finally, Zäria let out a sigh of relief. "So that's who Millie ran into."

"I wonder who this Thordon is and what he did to Millie," Avery said. "And why are the elves making all those chocolates? And why is it so secretive and guarded?"

"I don't know. Do you think we should tell Yamani?" Zäria hated going to Yamani for anything. The queen always did so much for her; she didn't want to be a bother.

Avery didn't answer right away. They flew in silence until Avery said, "I think we should think about it and decide what to do tomorrow."

"Tomorrow?" Zäria asked. "Why not go to Yamani right away?"

"It's not like anything is going to happen tonight."

"I guess you're right. I'll see you in the morning, then. It's already late."

"Okay. See you tomorrow." Avery waved and flew away home.

Zäria looked back toward Eerie Hollow and shrugged her shoulders. Her worries could wait until morning.

CHAPTER 3

Toadstools

When Avery got to his house, he saw a notice had been tacked with a clove to his door. It was from the Royal Order of Duty. He pulled it off the door and went inside, where he sat down and read the notice.

> The Royal Order of Duty hereby states that you, Avery Lightfoot, faerie son of Theadora and Aerion Lightfoot, from this day forward has the duty of caring for the toadstools of the forest. Be it known that failure to uphold your given duty will result in punishment, as declared by the queen of the realm.
>
> Report for your first day of training at first sight of faerie light on the morrow.
>
> Peevish Pollyweather III
> Faerie Overseer of Saizia

"Oh no!" Avery moaned. He had forgotten about the toadstools. It was far too late to get to Zäria tonight and let her know. He hoped he'd have time to tell her before leaving in the morning. All he wanted to do was fall into his bed and close his eyes. He put the letter aside, lay down on the dandelion-fluff bed, and pulled some fresh tree moss up to his nose. It was dark, and the sounds of the forest were quiet and soothing. Even though Avery was exhausted, however, he had a hard time falling asleep. There were too many things to think about. He was nervous about the toadstools, sorry he didn't have a chance to tell Zäria, worried about the elves in Eerie Hollow and what they were up to, and conflicted over what to do about it.

Avery woke up to the sound of a rapping and thudding noise. *Rap-rap-rap.* He didn't know how long he had slept. He only remembered tossing and turning and then, the next minute he was awake, and it wasn't dark anymore. *It must be morning,* he thought.

Rap-rap-rap.

But what was that noise? He blinked his eyes, trying to wake from this noisy dream. Then he realized it was the door. "Don't tell me I'm late for duty on the first day." He jumped from his bed and grabbed the closest thing to throw on himself before opening the door.

"Finally you answer the door. I've been knocking forever. Do you know what time it is? And why are you wearing your berry-gathering satchel like that?" Zäria was back to herself, talking fast as a bumblebee in spring.

Avery looked down at himself. What was he wearing? He brought his eyes back to Zäria. "I just grabbed the first thing I could get my hands on." He turned around and walked away as he was talking, leaving Zäria standing outside. He shouted from his room, "I'm sorry, Zäria. I didn't mean to leave you outside. Come in and close that door."

Avery threw on decent garb and returned to talk to Zäria. As he walked into the room, he saw her reading the notice from the Royal Order of Duty.

She placed the notice on the table and studied his attire. "That's much better."

"Zäria, I'm sorry. I forgot about the toadstools. We'll have to talk about Eerie Hollow when I get back."

"I understand. Don't apologize. I need to get to my duties as well. I remember my first day. You don't want to be late. They don't take it easy on the new faeries."

"Thanks. I'm really glad you're here. I thought I was going to have to leave without telling you. And I probably would have overslept too."

Her cheeks flushed and she softly giggled. "You don't have to report to me, Avery Lightfoot."

"You know that's not what I meant." The points of his ears turned red.

"Okay, okay. Just hurry up, and when you're done, meet me at Ladybug Landing. That's where I'll be eating lunch."

"I will. See you later. I really need to hurry." Zäria was already walking out the door when he added, "Oh, and Zäria ... don't tell anyone about the Hollow. We need to decide what to do before we get a bunch of faeries risking their wings out there."

"Yeah, I know. I'm not telling anyone." Zäria flapped her wings and took flight.

Avery watched her until he couldn't see her anymore; then he shut his door and made his way to the toadstools. He saw Mr. Beetle ahead of him, so he quickly darted behind a shrub on his right and took flight before Mr. Beetle saw him. He could still hear Mr. Beetle mumbling to himself. Avery shook his head and smiled as he passed. Mr. Beetle liked to chat, and chat, and chat, and he didn't seem to take "I'm late and need to go" as any sort of hint. Last time Avery had run into him, he had to endure almost an hour of hearing about the diverse types of fern within two feet of his house. It was not a favorite moment in his life.

It only took a minute or two for Avery to get to the toadstools. He saw three faeries flittering around from toadstool to toadstool, all girls. *Interesting,* he thought. He knew one of them, Flaira. She had golden-yellow hair in loops and curls, tied with grapevine tendrils. That's how he recognized her. He didn't know anyone else who wore her hair like that. He looked at the other two faeries, but they didn't look familiar to him. One was plump with long, wavy red hair that seemed to be in her way. The other was a little taller and thinner, with the blackest hair he'd ever seen. He thought she resembled a bumble bee in her bright yellow dress.

He decided to ask Flaira what he was to do. He flew over to the toadstools she was inspecting.

"Well, Avery Lightfoot. How nice of you to grace us with your presence and attend to your duty. You knew you were supposed to be here at first faerie light, didn't you? Mother will not be pleased with you."

"Uh … Mother?" Avery asked, confused.

"Yes, *my* mother. She is the Charge Faerie of the Toadstools." She pushed his arm to turn him around and pointed to her mother. She had wise eyes that were dark green, and her brown hair was pulled tightly into a bun. Even her wings looked precise and neat. "You need to talk to her," Flaira said, nudging him slightly.

Avery looked at Flaira and back at her mother with a perplexed look on his face. He did not want to move from his spot.

"Go, Avery."

"Ah, Okay. I mean … I was. I am." He took a deep breath and flew over.

Before he reached the charge faerie, she said, "You're late. Don't make that a habit." She barely looked up at him over the folder in her hand.

"Yes, I'm sorry," Avery said.

"Don't hover. My name is Persephani. You've met my daughter, Flaira." She pointed to the other two faeries. "That's Aduri in the yellow and Merry in green. They clean and heal the toadstools. Flaira harvests and stores them for winter. You will help her with all her duties."

"Should I go now?" Avery asked.

She lowered her folder and glared at him down the end of her nose. "You should have already been there, Avery. Do not waste my time again."

"Sorry; it won't happen again." He flew back over to Flaira, who was snacking on an acorn as she waited for him next to an oak tree.

Avery landed next to Flaira. "You knew I was going to be helping you, didn't you? Why didn't you just tell me?"

Flaira giggled and dropped her acorn. "Now what fun would that have been? Come on. We have a lot of catching up to do." Avery followed Flaira back to the toadstools as she explained, "We have to inspect all the toadstools and harvest the best. We store them for winter to make faerie soup and medicines." She felt the top and bottom of a toadstool cap.

"Wow, I didn't know the toadstools were so important," Avery said, bemused.

"All the faerie duties are important, silly. Each faerie is given his or her duty for a reason. Maybe you are supposed to learn something," Flaira explained.

"Yeah, maybe." He gave Flaira a confused look, which she seemed to ignore.

She went back to examining the toadstool. "It looks good enough for tinctures. Go ahead and harvest this one. You need to be careful not to pull the cap off the stem. I usually push them over to pull the root from the ground." She grabbed Avery's hands and put them on the toadstool. "Put your hands here at the top of the stem, under the gills."

Avery was surprised that she grabbed him and blushed at the touch of her soft, warm hands. He lost his balance, and the toadstool toppled over. He quickly flapped his wings and caught himself inches away from landing face-first in the mud.

Flaira laughed hard. "Oh, you rookie faeries never fail to entertain me."

Avery became even redder from embarrassment.

Flaira inspected the toadstool again. "At least you didn't damage it. Let's get this over to the storage while we're all still in one piece." She flew up and along the nearest tree.

How is that going to help me move this toadstool anywhere? Avery wondered.

Flaira pulled a leaf off the lowest branch and flew back down. "Here—roll the toadstool onto this leaf. I'll pull, and you keep it from rolling off."

Avery did what she asked. "Why didn't you just use a leaf off the ground?"

"The leaves on the ground are usually too weak. Besides this one is slightly diseased and needed to be plucked from the tree anyway." She pointed out the brown edges on the leaf she'd picked.

"Oh, that makes sense, I guess. Where is the storage?"

"It's over behind that mulberry bush." She grabbed the leaf's stem and started to pull the toadstool. It almost rolled off, but Avery caught it and held it still. When they got to the mulberry, Avery didn't see any storage. Then Flaira pulled a branch, and the whole bush moved backward and opened up the ground below to what looked like an underground cave. Then she rolled the toadstool into the hole and pulled the mulberry bush back over it.

"Doesn't that damage the toadstools, dropping them in a hole in the ground?" Avery asked.

"No. They roll down on a type of slide, and the storage faeries catch it at the bottom and take it from there. I can take you to see it later but not today. We're behind."

Another jab at me for being late? he wondered.

Flaira quickly darted off to a group of toadstools in a circle. "Never pick the toadstools growing in that formation. It's a faerie ring. A silly legend, but the elders take it seriously."

"Okay, no faerie rings."

"Now, this bunch over here is perfectly fine." She pointed to a mixed group of toadstools near a tree. "Let's see what you've learned."

Avery looked under the cap and around the stem. "I don't see any bruises or cuts. It looks healthy."

Flaira did her own inspection. "Yes, it will do."

Avery let out a sigh of relief that he'd gotten it right and hadn't looked foolish. He gently pulled the toadstool out of the ground but was horrified when the cap cracked, despite his best efforts. His face again flushed red with embarrassment.

Flaira put her hand on Avery's shoulder. "Not bad for your first harvest, Avery, but you'll have to learn to be more careful."

"I will."

They gathered up three more before Flaira said it was time to eat. Avery had been so busy that he hadn't thought of food. But now that she mentioned it, he was suddenly starving. He remembered he was supposed to meet Zäria for lunch but he couldn't leave now.

"I'll show you where we gather for meals," Flaira said as she flew off. Avery followed her through the trees to a small stream he had never seen before. Several faeries were there, enjoying lunch.

"So what would you like to eat?" Flaira asked. "It's customary for me to bring the newbie his first lunch, but don't get used to it. It's the one and only time. You can either bring lunch or buy it from Mrs. Bumblebee. She puts honey on everything." She smiled. "I packed a little extra today, just in case."

They sat down on a patch of moss. She had packed sunflower seeds, gooseberries, and lima beans. Avery didn't care for the lima beans, but he didn't dare complain. He popped a couple of sunflower seeds in his mouth and chewed them slowly while Flaira rambled on about something. Avery really didn't pay much attention to what she was saying.

Zäria sat at Ladybug Landing, impatiently waiting for Avery to join her. She was excited to hear about his first day. She had packed him all his favorite foods—blackberries, acorn muffins, and fennel. After a few minutes of waiting, her stomach started to growl. She'd been in such a rush that morning she'd forgotten to eat breakfast. Now, she wondered where Avery was.

Maybe I should bring his lunch to him, in case he's too busy working to leave, she thought.

When Zäria got to the toadstools, she didn't see Avery. She stopped a faerie to ask, "Do you know where I can find Avery Lightfoot? It's his first day."

"Don't know who he is," the faerie responded, "but you might want to check by the stream since it's lunchtime."

Zäria flew off in the direction the faerie pointed out.

It didn't take long for her to spot Avery. She headed toward him but then noticed he was sitting with a girl, eating lunch. *Did he forget he was supposed to have lunch with me? Who is that girl anyway?*

Zäria flew back home. She didn't even feel hungry anymore because she was humiliated and hurt.

The afternoon passed slowly for Zäria. She flew in circles inside her house; her mind was in a whirl, and she still wasn't sure why.

A knock on the door startled her. She opened it to find Avery. "Oh, it's just you," she said with a sniff.

"*Just* me? Are you waiting for somebody?" Avery asked.

"Not anymore." Zäria opened the door wider and let Avery walk inside. Then she slammed the door shut.

"What do you mean? Who *were* you waiting for? Hey, are those acorn muffins?" Avery said, taking everything out of the basket on the table. "I love acorn muffins and blackberries too."

Zäria quickly snapped the basket shut. "Avery Lightfoot, I know you love acorn muffins and blackberries. I packed that lunch for you, beetle brain."

"You did? Thanks."

"For lunch, Avery, remember? You were supposed to meet me at Ladybug Landing. When you didn't show, I brought it to you. Who was that faerie you ditched me for?" She was so angry she could hardly keep from shouting at him.

"You mean Flaira?" Avery asked.

Zäria rolled her eyes. "*Flaira,*" she repeated in a mocking tone.

"That's who I had to help all day with the toadstools. Why are you so mad?"

Zäria paused for a moment. "Because I put a lot of effort into packing your favorite foods, and you didn't even bother to show up."

"I'm sorry, Zäria. Can we eat it now?" Avery grabbed the basket and Zäria's hand. "Come on; it'll be like a picnic."

Now that she wasn't as angry anymore, she realized how hungry she was from skipping two meals that day. She finally gave in. "Okay. I'm starving."

They went outside and sat in the garden to eat. Avery ate two muffins and popped a blackberry in his mouth. "These are so good, Zäria. I didn't eat much for lunch. Flaira eats like a bird. Her lunch was just seeds, gooseberries, and lima beans. Yuck."

Zäria beamed at the thought of packing a better lunch than that

Flaira girl, but she was still annoyed that Avery had missed their lunch date. "Next time, show up for lunch, Avery."

"I said I was sorry," Avery said. "Now we have plenty of time to talk about Eerie Hollow. I think we should go back and find out more before we tell anyone."

"I don't know. It just seems dangerous. What if we get caught this time?"

"We won't get caught. We know where the elves are now, so we can be extra careful when we go in. I want to know why they're making all the chocolates. And maybe take some home. It looks delicious."

"How can you think about food when you've stuffed so much in your face already?" Zäria teased.

"I can always think about chocolate. Let's go after dark this time so it's easier to keep out of sight."

"Okay, Avery. But we tell the elders after this. Promise me."

"All right, I promise. First thing in the morning, we'll go see Yamani."

They shook hands to make it a deal.

CHAPTER 4

Chocolates

very helped Zäria clean up after their picnic. He wished there were a few more blackberries to eat. "Let's pick a few more berries before we go," he suggested.

"That's a good idea, Avery. We should gather items we might need in Eerie Hollow." Zäria picked up the basket and began to gather nuts and berries in the forest.

Avery had seen her do this a million times, but today he noticed how delicately she picked each berry, how the light shimmered through her golden-blonde hair. He shook the thoughts away and started gathering with her.

When the basket was full, they flew into Eerie Hollow side by side. Avery felt a bit more confident heading in this time. At least he had an idea of what they would find. When he started to smell the familiar scent of chocolate, he gently grabbed Zäria's hand and nudged her to land. He pulled her behind a nearby tree and held a finger to his mouth to shush her.

Avery peeked around the side of the large tree trunk to see if it was safe to proceed. He saw the same elves diligently working, along with a few others.

"Look," Zäria whispered, pointing to a figure dressed in dark robes. His hood blocked the view of his face but she assumed it was a man. He was taller than the elves, and he seemed to have a hunched back. The way the elves reacted to his presence showed that he was in charge.

"I bet that's Thordon—that's who the elves were talking about," Avery said. They watched the elves scurry around, seemingly trying to impress this mysterious dark figure. It was obvious the elves were intimidated by him. When he motioned for anything, the elves jumped over themselves to do what was asked. He appeared to be inspecting all the chocolate confections. After giving his approval, wagons full of chocolates were pulled farther into the forest.

Avery whispered, "Let's follow the wagons and see where they are taking all the chocolate."

Zäria nodded. Trying to be as quiet as possible, they went around several trees to get to the other side, where the wagons were lining up. Luckily, the elves were so busy and noisy that no one noticed the two faeries sneaking around, not even when Zäria's wing hit the crunchy dry leaves on a dead bush they were hiding behind. They silently followed the wagons through the forest and watched as, one by one, they went into a cave in the side of the mountain.

"Should we follow them in there?" asked Zäria.

"It looks dangerous. I'm not sure how we can get in without being seen, let alone get back out. And we don't know what's in there."

"I bet it's just storage for all those chocolates. How dangerous could that be?"

"We should be careful anyway." Avery watched the elves while trying to think of a plan. One of the wagons had stopped. It looked like a wheel had come loose after hitting a rock in the path. The two elves who were pushing the wagon were now busily tightening the wheel. Without a word, Avery quietly flew over and grabbed a couple of cloths and a basket of chocolates from the wagon. He was back before Zäria could argue.

"Are you crazy?" Zäria asked. "They could have seen you."

"They were too busy with the wheel." He handed one of the cloths to Zäria "Here—use this to hide your wings."

"Hide my wings?" she asked.

"Yeah, elves don't have wings. We won't have a chance of blending in with wings flapping in their faces."

Zäria noticed the basket of chocolates in Avery's hand. "Can I eat one of those? They smell divine." Zäria reached for a chocolate, but Avery quickly pulled the basket away.

"Not yet. We need these to get in the cave."

"We're going in there?" Zäria said, a little shakily.

"Yes. Now let's go. We'll walk alongside that wagon out of sight of the elves pushing it."

Zäria sighed in exasperation. "I sure hope you know what you are doing, Avery Lightfoot."

"Me too," Avery muttered to himself.

They stealthily moved around to the opposite side of the wagon and casually walked along, carrying the basket of chocolates. Once they crossed the opening of the cave, they slipped away into a dark crevice and waited for the elves and wagons to pass. Avery turned to whisper to Zäria and saw that she was stuffing a chocolate truffle in her mouth.

"Thms er da mush deshus chockesh eva," she mumbled with her mouth full.

"Zäria, you are gonna get us caught for sure." He popped a truffle in his mouth and then said, "O ma gush thesh er awshum."

Zäria held in a giggle as she held up her finger to her mouth. "Shhhh."

They wiped off the chocolate they had smeared on their hands and faces with their makeshift robes. Avery peeked out to make sure the coast was clear. Without a sound, he reached for Zäria, tugging her arm. They stepped out of their hiding spot and followed closely along a wall of the cave.

The mouth of the cave was rocky, damp, and dark, as expected, but the farther they moved in, the more it looked like a grand palace. The walls, floors, and ceilings sparkled with gems and shards of glass. The halls were lit with beautiful sconces housing hundreds of glowing fireflies. Avery had never seen anything like it.

They continued following the cave wall around in what felt like a giant circle, passing doorways and halls. Eventually they came to an opening much larger than the rest. Zäria and Avery both peeked around the corner. There was an enormous cavern, taking up most of the mountain's core. Elves, dwarfs, and other creatures were busily moving around in all directions. Some carried scrolls; others carried chocolates. But the main attraction was a giant dragon sitting at the far end of the room

Zäria gasped. Avery put his arm around her shoulder as he admired the majestic dragon. It had shiny, iridescent, yet velvety purple scales; a long, pointed tail; and silvery gossamer wings. Although Avery had never seen a dragon until now and even though it surely was the most enormous creature on the planet, he felt this must be the least intimidating dragon in history. It was gorgeous, and instead of breathing smoke and fire and gobbling up the small creatures, it was eating mounds and mounds of chocolate by the wagonful.

Avery whispered to Zäria, "Well, now we know what all that chocolate is for."

"Can you believe it?" Zäria asked. "I bet that dragon is as nice as can be. Maybe we should stop hiding and just introduce ourselves."

"Nice as can be? That's a dragon, Zäria. A larger-than-life, claws-bigger-than-both-of-us-together, giant sharp-teeth-chomping, fire-breathing dragon. And a dragon is a dragon."

"I could arrange for you to find out how nice a dragon can be, if you like," said a low, gruff voice from behind them.

They had been so focused on the dragon they hadn't been very cautious. The faeries both turned quickly on their heels and reflexively fluttered their wings in a panic, revealing they were fae under the robes.

Before them was the dark-robed figure from the woods, accompanied by a couple of creepy-looking dwarfs with axes. "But I, on the other hand, am not so nice," he said. "In fact ..." He motioned for the dwarfs to apprehend the two faeries, and the dwarfs then quickly shackled them. Avery didn't bother fighting. He knew they were caught.

"I've been described as downright nasty, along with a few other choice words. I am Thordon, and this cavern is off limits to all the fae. So are you enjoying your unsolicited tour thus far?"

Zäria said, "W-w-we just got l-lost and… and—"

"Got lost?" Thordon interrupted.

Avery nodded nervously. "We couldn't resist the sweet smell of the chocolates and followed the wagons here."

Thordon rubbed his chin. "Yes, the elves' delectable chocolates. They are not for sale, and we don't share." He turned his attention to the dwarfs. "Take them to the Lost Room, and let them really see what it means to be lost."

Thordon walked into the dragon's room with his robes trailing behind him as the dwarfs shuffled the two faeries back down the hall. Avery gagged from the smell of sweat and chocolate coming from the dwarfs. He tried to not breathe so deeply near them. One of the dwarfs pushed him forward, so Avery sped up a bit to keep his distance from them.

With all these twists and turns, Avery thought as they walked along the passageway, *it's hopeless—we'll never find our way out, even if we had the opportunity.* He definitely felt as lost as Thordon suggested. He was terrified but knew he needed to be strong for Zäria. He clasped her shaking hand in his.

The dwarfs grunted at the fae and motioned for them to stop in front of a large wooden door. It looked like any other door but without any visible hinges or handles. One of the dwarfs pulled a stone out of his pocket and tapped it on the door … and the door evaporated.

I didn't know elves or dwarfs had magic like us faeries, Avery thought.

He and Zäria were then pushed into the room, and just as suddenly as the door had disappeared, it reappeared again. From this side, the door looked strong and impenetrable. Instantly, Avery felt dizzy, as if the walls were closing in on him. He tried to regain his balance and reached out for Zäria, but she wasn't there.

"Zäria?" he shouted. Nothing. His vision had become slightly blurry, but he seemed to be surrounded by trees. He started to run, jumping over logs and dodging trees and shrubs. When he was out of breath and had a stitch in his side, he realized he was still two feet in front of that wooden door. Zäria was right next to him, breathing as heavily as he was. Apparently they'd both had the same experience. As soon as he started to get comfortable with his surroundings, it started again and then again. Sometimes he was in the woods, sometimes in a never-ending field.

In between episodes, Zäria collapsed in Avery's arms, weeping. "I was drowning in the pond, frantically splashing in the water, trying to keep my head above water and screaming for help."

He pushed his own fears aside and comforted her before the next episode began. After about a dozen of those horrifying episodes, the door suddenly evaporated again. Avery didn't know how long they had been trapped in that room. Tears streamed down both their faces. The overwhelming panic of being lost had taken its toll on them. Avery never thought he'd be relieved to see Thordon standing in front of them. He almost ran to hug him.

Thordon must have been expecting that reaction because he put his hands up in front of him to make sure Zäria and Avery kept their distance. His face displayed a creepy smirk as he asked, "So, my curious faeries, how 'lost' do you feel now?"

Avery tried to speak but it took a couple of tries to get it out. "Let us go home," he said with as much confidence and authority as he could muster.

"No, I think I will keep you a while longer. I rather enjoy your company. Elves are becoming a bore."

"What are you going to do with us?" Zäria asked, wiping the remaining tears from her face.

"I'm not going to do anything with you. You are simply going to be my … guests as we wait."

"Wait for what?" Avery asked.

"Your queen, Yamani. As we speak, an invitation is being delivered to your kingdom. I do hope your queen cares enough about you to come."

"She will come. And she'll bring warriors far greater than you!" Zäria spat out.

"I hope she does, but I wouldn't count on the warriors being so great."

Thordon disappeared down the hall. The dwarfs pulled Avery and Zäria out of the room, and they were once again herded down the hall, this time into a smaller room. The door opened and closed normally, and the inside had solid stone walls and floors. It looked ordinary enough to be safe.

Silly thing to hope for a prison cell to be safe, Avery thought, *but considering the room we just left, this is a significant improvement.* He collapsed to the floor from exhaustion, with Zäria beside him.

The floor was cold and damp. They nestled together for warmth and tried to sleep, but Avery couldn't keep his eyes closed for long. Every noise startled him, and he had nightmares of the lost room. Without a window in the room, Avery could not tell if it was day or night or how many hours they had been in the room.

When sleep became a chore, Avery paced back and forth across the small room. His only choice was to wait and wonder about their fate. He didn't know how he could protect Zäria in this place and felt a bit hopeless. He looked at her huddled in a ball on the cold floor. He saw her twitch as if she was having a nightmare, and he kneeled down to comfort her. He hoped Yamani would bring them home.

G E

CHAPTER 5

Visitors

Gus marched down Caterpillar Galley to Yamani's palace, accompanied by the twins, Sprout and Bean. He took in the peacefulness of the forest to calm his nerves. He listened to the fireflies as they hummed and buzzed, and he watched them flutter freely through the cool, crisp air. Gus heard the patter of scurrying insects around them, soft and rhythmic in the darkness.

He had never been to Saizia and was overwhelmed by its beauty. He noticed the path was lined with colorful flowers, and he smelled the scent of lavender in the air, which gave him the false sense that nothing was amiss. However, he began to see several faeries peeking out their doors and windows to gawk at them. His nerves came back as some fae had even started following along behind him to the palace. He suspected they had never seen elves in Saizia and were just curious.

When the elves reached the gates, guards were at the ready, with spears in hand. Gus cleared his throat and tried to speak with a confident voice. "We have an important message for Queen Yamani."

One of the guards walked back up the steps and through the palace doors without a word. He returned rather quickly and spoke without emotion to the elves. "The queen will see you now. Come with me." The other guards opened the gates and led them to the court at the bottom of the steps, where a guard motioned for them to wait.

The guards positioned themselves on either side of Gus and the twins. Gus jumped slightly when the horns sounded to announce the queen. Yamani appeared through the entrance, surrounded by guards, attendants, and members of the court. It was an intimidating scene. The elves waited silently in awe. Gus thought the faeries truly were beautiful and graceful creatures.

Yamani was decorated in gardenia petals. She definitely looked royal to the portly elf. She was dressed completely in white, and the aroma of gardenia was intoxicating.

When Yamani reached her throne, she turned and acknowledged the three nervous elves. All who followed her then bowed and knelt down around their queen. Gus looked around and clumsily followed suit; he started to bow. When he noticed that Bean and Sprout were still standing, awestruck, he slapped them both on their backs. They quickly bowed as well.

While all heads were now bowed, Yamani addressed the court. "Please rise." Once the elves raised their heads and were facing her, she continued. "What is the message you have traveled to deliver and from whom?"

The elves absentmindedly looked at each other as Gus fumbled with the scroll. He read aloud. "Dear Queen Yamani and all of Saizia, despite a century-old pact, yet another incident of trespassing in Eerie Hollow has occurred. This grievance will not be resolved by a magical vow of silence." Gus was taken aback by the sea of gasps that erupted from the onlooking faeries, and he paused for a moment, cleared his throat, and then continued. "The offenders of this pact will be confined in the dungeon of Eguin until the next blue moon, at which time their wings will be removed, and they will become our eternal slaves."

Once again Gus was interrupted by the audience reaction of shock and fear, and it spread through the crowd. When he looked around, the faeries became silent so he could go on.

"The new price for trespassing in Eerie Hollow will be death, as decreed in the Pact of Elders and executed by the kingdom of Eerie Hollow. Lord Thordon." Gus rolled up the scroll and looked up at the queen, awaiting her response.

Yamani did not look pleased with this news. She looked out among the faeries and spoke to them. "Fear not, my faeries. There is indeed such a pact among the faeries and the elves, bound over one hundred years ago. It was formed to prevent the union between the two colonies. A union between elves and faeries almost always resulted in children becoming outcasts, considered as mutant deformities, not belonging to the elves or the faeries. They would have wings but would not be able to fly, or they were exceptionally small, like wingless pixies. I do believe that Thordon himself was a result of an elf-faerie union."

Yamani made her way to her throne and sat down. "My mother made that pact so long ago I'd nearly had forgotten about it. I'd also almost forgotten that the elves were living so near our home in Eerie Hollow—until late one night, when Millie Whisperwing was brought to my palace by Thordon himself. He was frantically upset that she had been, as he said, 'snooping' around his forest. Although I felt it truly was a harmless accidental encounter, we agreed that we must protect the pact and keep the elves a secret to keep further disturbances from occurring. I had the vow of silence placed on Millie to protect all of the faeries, including her. We allowed all of you to believe that she was scared voiceless out of Eerie Hollow because it was haunted. It was our hope that no other faeries would wander inside for fear of the same fate. This pact was never meant to be taken so seriously that innocent faeries would be punished by mutilation or death."

She paused for a few moments. All the faeries and even the elves were silent, trying to take it all in and make sense of it. Yamani turned back and addressed the elves. "I intend to accompany you to Eerie Hollow and speak to Thordon in person. This is not a matter that can be resolved by messenger."

Gus hesitated while trying to think of a response. Thordon had not prepared him for the possibility that the faerie queen would want to return with them. Faeries were not allowed in Eerie Hollow. He might pay the price for her visit. Finally, he said cordially, "Queen Yamani, we'd be most obliged to advise Lord Thordon you wish to request a meeting with him."

"No," Yamani snapped. "I will not give him warning and time to prepare for my arrival. I will bestow the same courtesy to him that he has bestowed upon me. You will accept I have enough courage to deliver my own message."

Sprout and Bean looked at Gus. Sprout said quietly to the other elves, "Maybe we should do as she says. She *is* the queen."

"She is the queen of the fae, not the elves," Bean shot back.

"I don't think we have a choice," Gus said. "The penalty will be high, no matter what our decision." He took a deep breath and reluctantly agreed. "We will show you the way to Thordon, but we must ask that you limit your entourage to only three guards, attendants, or advisers."

"Three?" Yamani said, outraged. "I am to travel with such limited security during such a conflict—and into the home of my aggressor, no less?"

"The penalty we may face for bringing a faerie to our home is great, and we are only making an exception for Your Highness. We are at notable risk in doing you this favor. Please do us the favor of not making it appear we have brought an opposing army to the door," Gus said respectfully.

Yamani paused as if to consider his request. "Very well," she said, though she was clearly frustrated. "Please make yourselves at home while I prepare for our journey. I will be but a few moments. You may enjoy a bite to eat in my absence." She motioned for her attendants to come forward. "Please make our guest comfortable. Bring them food and drink."

The attendants nodded and flew off to get to work. Yamani removed herself from her throne and returned to the palace.

The elves were taken to a small table in a garden, where they were given toast with acorn butter, gooseberries, and pumpkin tea. Bean and Sprout seemed to enjoy all the fluttering faeries who showered them with attention. Gus, however, was very worried and distant. He barely sipped his pumpkin tea and didn't touch a bite of food. He looked out at all the faeries still gathered around; they looked back at him with mixed emotions.

"They sure are beautiful, aren't they, Gus?" Sprout asked, breaking the uncomfortable silence.

"Who?" Gus said absentmindedly.

"The faeries," Sprout said. "Every last one of them is beautiful and graceful too." He looked at them with admiration.

While watching the busy faeries, Bean said, "I wish I could fly. Think how fast we could get all our work done."

"Yeah," agreed Sprout rather dreamily.

Gus was thankful a ladybug came up to the table and ended their babbling.

She spoke softly. "I'm Lillie, one of Queen Yamani's attendants. She has advised that she is now ready to depart. Please come with me."

The three elves followed Lillie back to the palace, where they found Yamani, two guards, and a young faerie waiting for them. Gus felt Yamani was less conspicuous in a hooded brown cloak, and he was glad her guards did not appear to be fully armed.

"We are ready when you are," Yamani advised.

"Let's get a move on, then. It's a long walk." Gus turned to the queen, realizing she could fly. "Are you sure you want to walk, Your Highness?"

"Yes, we will walk with you on this trip." She put her arm out in a shooing motion. "Come, come. Let's go. We have held you up long enough."

The group started off down Caterpillar Galley, which now was lined with faeries. A couple of faerie children followed them to the end of the galley, giggling, half skipping, and half flying.

It didn't take long for the group to reach the outskirts of Saizia. Eerie Hollow was nearly in sight, but it would be nightfall before their arrival.

"Your Highness, do you need to rest?" Gus asked. "Are you sure you wouldn't rather fly?"

The queen took a moment to answer and then said, "It does seem much farther and more laborious to walk, but if I fly, I'll get there before you. As my visit is unannounced and probably unwelcome, I would prefer to arrive with you so that you can announce my presence as not being a threat." The queen's attendant was struggling to carry Yamani's trailing robe when the queen suddenly stopped. "Perhaps a short rest wouldn't hurt. I would like something to drink."

The group stopped for a few minutes while the queen's attendant brought a goblet of water to her. Everyone else got their own drink of water. Once Yamani was ready, they set off again.

Bean said, "It won't really be that long. We'll be in Eguin's cavern before you know it."

"Eguin's cavern?" the queen repeated. "I thought we were going to see Thordon in Eerie Hollow."

Gus smacked Bean in the back of the head.

"What?" Bean asked, rubbing his head.

Gus tried to correct Bean's blunder. "We are going to see Thordon. Bean shouldn't have brought up the cavern because we will not be going there." He gave Bean a keep-your-mouth-shut look.

"What is this Eguin?" Yamani asked. "The name was also mentioned in the message you delivered. Eguin's dungeon and now Eguin's cavern. I have never heard of it before."

Gus didn't answer right away; he wasn't sure what to tell her. He decided to be as vague as possible. "They are just places in Eerie Hollow."

"I see," she said.

When they reached the edge of Eerie Hollow, the elves continued on and walked right in, while Yamani and her guards stopped. Yamani's attendant nearly ran into the queen, not expecting the sudden stop. Gus noticed no one was following him and doubled back to see what happened. He came around some trees and found the faeries dumbstruck and staring at the woods.

Behind Gus, Sprout whispered to Bean, "Do you think they are scared or something?"

"I don't know," Bean replied.

Gus held up a hand to signal the twins to keep quiet. "Is something wrong, Queen Yamani?" Gus asked.

The queen looked startled, as if she'd been in deep thought. She looked at the three elves and then her faeries. "Oh no," she sighed.

"It's just been so long since I've been here. It almost doesn't look the same."

"You've been here before? Faeries aren't allowed here," Sprout blurted.

"I was here before that." She waved them on. "Please, let's continue."

They all carried on, walking into the hollow, dry leaves and twigs cracking and crunching under their feet. After a few moments, Gus noticed the guards twitching their noses and sniffing the air. Then the queen's attendant started to do the same thing. He had forgotten about the chocolate and had brought them too close. He could see they were already curious.

The queen asked, "Why are you all acting so peculiar?"

"Don't you smell it, Your Highness?" one of the guards asked.

"The …"—her attendant stopped to sniff—"chocolate. That's it. Chocolate!"

"Chocolate? Here?" Yamani sniffed the air.

Gus knew that bringing the queen of the faeries here would prove a bad idea. He sent a worried glance to Bean and Sprout. He had to act fast. "Hmm, perhaps Your Majesty should wait here with your entourage while Bean and I announce your arrival? We'll investigate this … uh … chocolate aroma as well," he suggested.

"Very well. I am a little tired of walking. Please do be prompt, though. I do not like to be kept waiting."

"Sprout, please look after our guests, and for their safety, do not bring them any farther into Eerie Hollow. We wouldn't want to cause an uproar if other elves were to see them."

"Yes, yes. I will stay here with them," Sprout replied distractedly. He watched as the queen took a seat on a nearby toadstool and her attendant handed her a vial of sunflower nectar to drink. The guards stood by the queen and kept a lookout in all directions.

Sprout paced back and forth, not really sure what to do with the faerie queen while they waited for Gus to return. The young faerie attendant took a seat on a stone next to Sprout. Nervously, he asked, "Uh, what is your name? I don't remember anyone saying."

She looked up at him and smiled sweetly. "Attendants are not customarily introduced to anyone while in the presence of the queen. But since you asked, my name is Poppy."

"Poppy," he repeated. "Interesting."

"What do you mean, interesting?" she asked and then took a sip of nectar.

"I don't know. I just think your name is interesting. Like the flower. I like it." He realized he must have made her uncomfortable because she looked over at the queen.

"I should go see if Yamani needs anything else," she said.

Embarrassed, Sprout replied, "Oh, yes, yes. Go ahead and do that. I didn't mean to bother you."

He admired her as she flapped her wings and gracefully fluttered over to the queen. Sprout leaned against a tree and tapped his foot, suddenly feeling like this was going to be a long wait. He looked over at the queen's guards, who were watching the forest around Yamani with great intent.

Once Poppy was finished fussing over the queen, she returned to Sprout and sat down next to him. "It's kind of nice to have somebody to talk to, ya know?" she said.

"Oh yeah. Sure." *Maybe waiting won't be so bad after all*, he thought. He coyly inched a bit closer to the faerie on the rock.

"So where do you think that chocolate smell is coming from?" Poppy asked.

Without thinking, he quickly replied, "It's coming from the chocolate mines, of course."

"Chocolate mines?"

"Well, they're not really mines. More like storages. The elves make all sorts of things with chocolate. So we have to store a lot," Sprout said.

"Then why did that other elf, Gus, act like he didn't know?"

Sprout, finally realizing he wasn't supposed to say, tried to cover up his goof. "Oh, you know, Gus is a little ..." He motioned with his hand to his head, implying that Gus was not all there.

Poppy giggled. "So you must really like chocolate."

"Well yeah, but when you work with it all day, it's the last thing you want to eat."

"I feel that way too sometimes."

"About chocolate or the queen?"

They both laughed, which got the queen's attention. Yamani glowered at them, and they quickly stopped laughing and tried to regain their composure.

The guards suddenly stood up straight and looked in the direction from which Gus had left.

In the distance, Sprout saw Gus walking toward them, followed by Thordon and a few elfin guards. Sprout turned to look at Yamani, who was now standing, flanked by her guards. Poppy took her place behind the queen. Sprout backed out of Thordon's way when he arrived to allow him speak to the queen.

He bowed slightly to her. "Ah, Yamani, it's an ineffable pleasure to see you, as always."

Sprout did not think Yamani appeared flattered by his greeting.

"Thordon, as you know, this is not a cordial dinner visit. I am here to deliver a response to your message. I am less than pleased with your actions against my faeries."

"My actions? Against your faeries?" He scoffed. "And what of their violation?"

"Those faeries were ignorant of the violation to the pact."

"How could they not know about a pact that has been in place for over one hundred years?" Thordon said, throwing up his hands.

"They do not know because we stopped teaching about it many years ago. The faeries were not tempted to go to Eerie Hollow because they did not know about it."

Thordon shook his head. "That, Yamani, is very careless and is the cause of your current predicament."

"I did not come here to get advice on how to rule my kingdom. I am here to collect my faeries and bring them home."

"Ignorance is no excuse for breaking laws and violating pacts. Their freedom will come with a price."

"What price would that be?" Yamani asked, exasperated.

"There is something I need from the Perilous Forest. I will let them go back to your kingdom without harm, once it's in my hands."

"Zäria and Avery could not possibly be capable of such a dangerous journey. They've never been outside the forest of Saizia."

"If that were true, they wouldn't be in my charge. That is the offer. They either go on the quest for me, or they remain my slaves. If they survive the quest, they go free. If not ... well, then, they've paid their debt."

"What is so important that my faeries must travel such a great distance to retrieve it?"

"Don't worry; it's nothing dangerous. Just a mere seed," Thordon explained.

"You expect two young faeries to risk their wings for a seed? That is absurd, Thordon. Send one of your own elves, and give back my faeries at once!"

Sprout was reminded of when Thordon had sent him and Bean to fetch the seed. Even with the map, they just ended up going in circles through the Perilous Forest. He never wanted to set foot in that forest again.

"I've tried that already. It must be a faerie. You should accept my offer; it's the only choice I'm giving you."

"Whatever it is, I'm sure my faerie guards can find it and bring it to you. I can't bear to see my young fae harmed."

"No, this is a special quest for the captured faeries to earn their freedom."

Yamani was silent for a moment.

Sprout was curious about the strange tension between Yamani and Thordon. He had never seen Thordon allow anyone to argue with him.

"I wish to speak to the faeries first," Yamani finally said, "and let them decide their own fate. Take me to them, and if they feel they are up for the challenge, then so be it."

Thordon gave a crooked grin. "Very well. You may see them. I cannot allow you to go any farther into the hollow; I will have them brought here." He gestured to the guard on his left. The guard walked away and a few moments later returned with a wagon. Sprout figured Thordon must have expected Yamani's request because Zäria and Avery stepped out of the wagon, both looking confused and distraught.

Avery and Zäria bowed to their queen after they were placed in front of her.

"Please rise," Yamani said. "We have an important matter to discuss." Zäria and Avery stood up and raised their heads. "I don't have time to provide much detail, but it is time you knew about the ancient pact between the faeries and the elves. It has been agreed for a century that neither will trespass in the other's home. Because of your breach of this pact, you risk the severe consequences of losing your wings and remaining slaves to the elves in Eerie Hollow."

The two faeries gasped and looked at each other in shock. Both started to object but Yamani shushed them.

"Thordon has taken into consideration your ignorance of the pact and has offered an alternate fate. He has set forth a quest to retrieve a seed from the Perilous Forest."

"We'll do it," Avery blurted.

"Anything," Zäria added.

Yamani shook her head. "The journey to the Perilous Forest is extremely treacherous. You will not be allowed to bring along trained guards and will need to risk these dangers on your own."

"Queen Yamani," Avery said, "if it's a choice between losing our wings and delivering a seed, we'll take the seed."

Zäria nodded in agreement; she loved her wings.

"This is not just some pathetic seed you are to retrieve," Thordon spat. "It is very important, and you will need to risk your lives to remove it from the Perilous Forest. And remember: even if you make it back alive, you will need to deliver the seed to gain your freedom. If I don't get my seed, I will have your wings, and your queen won't save you."

"Thordon, I need a word with the faeries in private, please. Would you mind?" She shooed him away and then motioned for Zäria and Avery to come close.

Sprout wondered what she was saying, but she whispered so quietly, he couldn't hear a thing.

Yamani turned back to Thordon. "I'm sure you would not oppose allowing the faeries supplies for their journey?"

"Of course not, but make it quick. They need to set off at once."

"Poppy." Yamani waved her attendant to come closer to her.

"Yes, Your Highness."

"Give the faeries all the provisions you have brought with you. We will make due, and they have more need of it."

Sprout watched as Poppy quickly gathered up her satchels filled with food and drink and gave them to Zäria.

"Guards, give the faeries any survival gear you can spare."

The guards started pulling out small weapons, armor, and tools. The faeries took everything and packed it in one of Poppy's satchels.

"I'm sorry we could not offer more. We packed light for our short journey and were not expecting yours."

"We are more than grateful for your kindness," Zäria said, curtsying to the queen.

On Thordon's order, the elfin guards escorted the faeries back to the wagon. Once the wagon pulled away, Thordon addressed the queen once more. "Now that this is settled and is up to the faeries to make up for their mistake, I regretfully must bid you adieu." With that, he turned and walked away.

The elves looked among each other, shrugged, and followed Thordon. Sprout turned to look at Poppy one last time before he followed the other elves.

CHAPTER 6

Zäria

While surrounded by cheering fae, Avery's parents, Theadora and Aerion, watched as the queen and her company reached the gate to the palace. Theadora stopped cheering when she noticed that Avery and his friend Zäria were not with the queen. She shushed the faeries around her and waited for the queen to tell them what had happened to the young fae. Instead, the queen passed the faeries and walked up the palace steps.

Before Yamani reached the door, Theadora Lightfoot shouted desperately, "Where are Avery and Zäria, my queen? Why have they not returned with you? Were they hurt or … or …" She dropped to her knees and sobbed. Aerion tried to comfort her and helped her up.

Queen Yamani paused for a moment, sighed, and then continued into the palace. One of the guards announced to the crowd, "The queen is fatigued from her journey. A meeting with the kingdom will be called once she has rested. Until then, please carry on with your normal duties. Thank you." He too turned and disappeared into the palace.

Theadora asked Aerion, "How could Yamani be so cruel to not to tell a poor mother the fate of her only son?" She sobbed into her hands.

"I do not know. I'm sure she had her reasons. We can only hope Avery and Zäria are safe and will be home soon."

Theadora leaned on Aerion for strength to help her walk home.

Persephani and Flaira stood in the crowd nearby. They felt bad for the Lightfoots as they watched them fly home, clearly disheartened and worried.

"It appears you won't have any help with your work in the morning, Flaira," Persephani advised. "I knew that faerie was a troublemaker, showing up late on the first day and now disappearing into Eerie Hollow. I hope, for Theadora's sake, they return home."

"So do I. Avery is a good faerie. I haven't met Zäria. Were her parents here too?"

"Zäria's parents are unknown. She was found near the hollow and brought here by one of the queen's maids long ago. Yamani named her and ordered all the fae to help raise her. There really wasn't a lot of discussion about where she came from. Everyone just felt the need to care for her and to help her feel that she belonged here."

"That is really sad," said Flaira. "I wonder why she was in the hollow alone."

"That's about the time that the pact was initiated," Persephani said. "Yes, a council meeting was held, and the announcement was made that no faerie would be allowed to enter Eerie Hollow and vice versa. Fae and elves were not to communicate any further. I remember Yamani being so upset after her mother announced the pact."

"Why is that, Mother?"

"She went to Eerie Hollow regularly, nearly every day. I'm sure that's how she found Zäria."

"I wonder if that had something to do with starting the pact."

"That very well may be true, Flaira. Come now; let's get some rest. I hope Queen Yamani will shed some light on this whole state of affairs."

The following morning, Theadora and Aerion waited outside the palace gates for the queen's announcement. Persephani, Flaira, and some of the others from the toadstools were standing near them. Flaira put her hand on Theadora's shoulder. "I hope Avery is okay."

"Thank you, Flaira," Theadora replied with tears in her eyes.

The chattering crowd hushed when two guards marched out of the palace and to the bottom of the steps. They posted themselves on either side of the queen's throne. Three of her faeries-in-waiting were the next to exit the palace. They stood directly next to the throne.

The queen's adviser announced, "Please hold silent for Queen Yamani."

At that, Yamani walked out of the palace. She was adorned in blue forget-me-not petals. Her hair was tangled into a bun on top of her head and was circled by a crown of daisies and lavender.

Theadora held her breath and bit her lip, expecting to hear the worst.

Yamani remained standing as she spoke to the fae of her kingdom. "As you all know, last night I visited Eerie Hollow with the intention of bringing home two of our faeries, Avery and Zäria."

Theadora grasped Aerion's arm a little tighter in anticipation.

"Thordon was keeping them prisoner and fully intended to cause them harm. Instead, he gave them the option of undertaking a quest; if they refused, however, they would lose their wings and become his slaves."

The crowd of faeries gasped in shock. Chatter and whispers started to spread. Then shouts of "Lose their wings?" and "This means war!" and "Who does that elf think he is?"

This added to Theadora's panic. She brushed the tears from her eyes. "Yamani, where has he sent my Avery?"

Queen Yamani waved to the crowd to hush. "Thordon has sent them to the Perilous Forest."

"The Perilous Forest?" Theadora cried. "That is a dangerous journey. How could you agree to this?"

"Avery and Zäria made the choice of their own accord. Saying no meant they would lose their wings and be eternal slaves. Taking the risk of the quest meant a chance to return home unharmed. I wanted to allow them a chance. I provided them with a few supplies to aid them in their journey."

"Why didn't you send them with guards?" Theadora asked.

"Thordon wouldn't allow it. I'm sorry, Theadora. I share your worries and heartache."

"How could you possibly understand the worries and heartache of a mother?" Theadora snapped. Then she realized how cruel and disrespectful she had been to her queen, and she gasped, throwing a hand to her mouth.

"There is another secret that has been kept from Saizia for far too long. The pact was created because of me." Yamani sat on her throne. "I was a young, curious princess. My mother and father went to great pains to tame me. One of my favorite adventures was to visit Eerie Hollow and spend my days with the elves. They were so different from the fae and made for a lot of entertainment. I made a friend who was part elf and part faerie. I couldn't get enough of finding out about him—he had wings but could not fly and had a little bit of faerie magic." She paused for a moment or two, as though trying to remember. The crowd was silent, waiting to know the truth.

"He became so much more than a friend," Yamani said. "We came to the king and queen to ask to be wed. My father was enraged over the mere idea of it. He said the union of elf and faerie was unheard of. I argued that he was faerie too. But I could not get my parents' blessing. I ran away to Eerie Hollow. There, we had an elven ceremony. I did not returned to Saizia for a year or more. When we had a child of our own, I decided it was time to return. I brought her to meet my mother and father. They did not acknowledge my union or my child. My mother, the queen, announced the next day that I had found the child in the hollow as an orphan. The pact was created, and I was to remain in the forest and take my place as queen, or I would never see Zäria again." The queen had tears in her eyes.

Taken aback, Theadora asked, "Zäria ... is your child, Queen Yamani? Does that also mean that Thordon ..." She could not bring herself to say the words.

"Yes," the queen replied. "Thordon is Zäria's father."

A faerie from the crowd shouted, "Does he know this?"

All waited for the queen's response.

"He only knows we had a child. He does not know it is Zäria. He is very bitter that I never returned to him. He is determined to hurt the fae, as he feels we have hurt him." She stood and walked to Theadora. When they were face-to-face, she grabbed Theadora's hands in hers. "I share your worry and heartache—I have for years. I envy your being able to raise your child as your own."

Theadora rested her head on their clasped hands. "Please forgive my harsh words, Your Majesty. There has to be something Your Majesty can do to protect them in some way."

"I have advised the young fae to seek out the faerie sanctuary when in need."

Theadora lifted her head to look at the queen. "I forgot about the sanctuary. Did you give them a faerie stone?"

"I regret that I did not have one with me to give. They will have to journey through the Perilous Forest and rely on the faerie magic of the sanctuary to help them." The queen let go of Theadora's hands and returned to her throne. "I urge all the faeries to please return to your duties and await the young faeries' return. Worry will not bring them home to us. I have faith in Avery and Zäria, for they are both clever young fae," advised the queen.

Yamani then signaled to her guards that she was ready to leave. The guards followed her into the palace.

Theadora was relieved that Avery was no longer a prisoner in Eerie Hollow but scared for the risks he and Zäria would face in the Perilous Forest. She took comfort in the strength of the sanctuary's faerie magic; it would protect them.

CHAPTER 7

The Pact

Zäria was cold and cramped after being kept in Thordon's wagon overnight. She snuggled up to Avery to keep warm while he slept. She tried to get some sleep but was startled awake when the door squeaked open. Zäria woke Avery, and the two climbed out of the wagon to find Thordon waiting for them. He handed them a rolled-up piece of paper.

"That map will show you the way to the Perilous Forest. The seed you are looking for is somewhere in that forest. There is a picture of it on the map."

"What kind of seed is it?" Zäria asked.

"That is not of your concern," snapped Thordon.

"Well, it would make it easier to find if we knew what type of plant it will grow into," Avery said.

"This seed hasn't been planted for many, many years, and there are no growing plants anymore. I have given you all I am prepared to offer; the rest is up to you. Good luck, and don't let anything happen to that seed." With that, Thordon turned his back to them and walked away. His entourage took the cue to follow suit.

Avery and Zäria watched them disperse for a few moments, and then he said, "The sooner we go, the sooner we get home."

"I hope you're right. Home sounds really good right now." They quickly looked through their supplies and made sure everything was packed well for their journey. "We should gather some food first. We don't know what will be available or safe to eat where we're going," said Zäria.

"Good idea. I'll pick some nuts from the trees, and you can gather herbs and berries." Avery handed her an empty satchel that Poppy had given them.

Once Zäria's satchel was full, she and Avery started out on their journey. The map Thordon had given them looked ancient, and Zäria hoped it was still accurate. They took off in the direction of the Perilous Forest, flying over the trees for a better view. Zäria could see for miles; it was clear this was going to be a long trip.

After a few hours, Avery said to Zäria, "My wings are getting tired, and I'm hungry. Let's find a place to rest for a moment."

"Sounds good to me. I'm ready to rest too."

"Let's stop over there by that pond." He pointed down to a small green pond lined with raspberry bushes. When they landed, Zäria said she would pick some of the berries, but Avery stopped her. "No, we don't know they're safe."

"They are just raspberries, Avery."

"I don't want to take the chance of eating things we didn't bring with us." He pointed at the map. "I think we are in the Witch's Swamp. We need to take extra precautions."

"Very wise," said an unfamiliar voice. The faeries turned toward the voice and found it was a crow. The sleek black bird was perched on a tree stump, stretching its wings. It continued to talk. "Those berries have been poisoned by a witch. Eat a few of those, and you will fall asleep so she can capture you and take you to her coven."

"Why should we believe you?" asked Avery.

"Doesn't matter. You can go ahead and eat them and find out for yourselves. On the other hand, heeding my warning won't hurt you at all."

"I guess we just won't eat them to be on the safe side," Zäria said.

"Safe side?" the crow asked. "There is no safe side. You are in the Witch's Swamp. I wouldn't stay long."

Zäria thought the crow wanted to be helpful, so she decided to be friendly and polite. "We were just stopping to rest, and then we'll be on our way. What's your name?"

The crow ruffled its feathers and puffed up a bit. "My name is Weezelbet. Where are you going?"

"The Perilous Forest," answered Avery.

"Intriguing," said Weezelbet. "What's your business in the Perilous Forest?"

"That's not important," Avery said.

"The Perilous Forest is cursed and is very dangerous, so it must be important if you are risking going there."

"Cursed?" Zäria looked to Avery. "No one said anything about a curse."

"I must know. What is worth risking your lives?" said Weezelbet with a curious expression.

Zäria whispered to Avery, "Maybe we can ask if Weezelbet knows where to find the seed."

"Seed? Interesting. I remember some elves coming by here looking for a seed too. Unfortunate fools. They didn't listen to my warning; they ate two handfuls each of those poisoned berries. Witches took them. Must be a pretty amazing seed."

"I think we should go before the witches come." Avery lightly tugged on Zäria's arm.

"Too late," said Weezelbet. Sparks shot from a purple puff of smoke, and a witch suddenly stood where the crow had been.

Zäria gasped. "If you're a witch, why did you warn us about the berries?"

The witch laughed. "Those berries aren't poisoned. I tricked you, so you'd spill your guts. And spill, you did. I want this seed you are looking for, whatever it is."

"We don't even know what it is," said Avery.

"You're going into the most dangerous forest to get a seed, and you don't even know what it is? Lies!" yelled the witch.

"We are telling the truth. We had no choice but to go," Avery retorted.

"Who is forcing you to go?"

"Thordon of Eerie Hollow," Zäria replied, although she wasn't sure why she was answering a witch.

The witch started pacing back and forth and muttering angrily about elves and broken promises—something that Zäria couldn't quite make out. Weezelbet suddenly looked up and said, "You will take me with you."

"Take you?" Zäria asked.

"Why would we take a witch with us?" Avery asked.

"You will take me with you, or I will take you back to the coven and let the elder witches decide what to do with you."

"Why haven't you done that already?" Zäria asked.

"I find you intriguing. I haven't seen faeries in centuries. I want to know what is so important about this seed. And Thordon owes me a debt. Besides, you will need someone who has been to the Perilous Forest in order to survive it."

"A witch wants to help us?" Avery said, not sure he believed it.

Insulted, she said, "Just because I'm a witch doesn't mean I'm evil and untrustworthy."

Zäria and Avery looked at each other. Avery asked, "How do we know we can trust you?"

"How do you know you can trust anyone? Have I brought you to harm?" asked the witch.

Zäria thought about it for a moment. "No, but you did threaten us."

"I merely gave you a choice," Weezelbet said as she picked at her crooked green-tinted nails.

"Not a very good one," Zäria said.

"It's still a choice, nonetheless."

Avery sighed. "We will take you. We must return this seed. We can't give up at the first sign of trouble."

"You are smart!" Weezelbet exclaimed.

"I hope we don't regret this. I can't believe we are taking a witch on this journey," said Zäria. *Avery must be crazy for agreeing to this,* she thought, *but I guess it's the only option.*

"Watch your tongue, faerie. I will not be mocked," the witch said as she turned back into the black crow. "This will make it easier to travel with you," Weezelbet advised.

"That's going to take some getting used to," said Avery.

The faeries and the witch-crow started on the journey to the Perilous Forest. They flew until dusk, and then Avery said, "We need to find a place to stop for the night."

"Afraid of a little darkness, are we?" cackled Weezelbet.

"No, we can't see where we're going in the dark, and we need to sleep," Avery said. "Don't witches sleep?"

"Not with both eyes closed," replied the witch.

Zäria pointed to the forest below. "Those trees over there look like a good spot."

"Trees? I'm not sleeping in a tree," the witch-crow said.

"Then don't," Avery said sharply.

"You don't have to be rude. There's an inn not far from here. You can sleep in a warm bed there."

"A human inn?" asked Avery. "We can't stay there. They would trap us."

"I'm a witch, remember?" Weezelbet said as she flew down, landed on the ground, and quickly changed back into a witch. "I can get a room and hide you."

"They aren't going to let a witch in either," Zäria said.

"Tsk-tsk. I don't have to look like a witch. I can be a little girl." She suddenly changed into a little girl with blonde braids. "Or a farmer." She then turned into a burly man with a long beard. "Or a grandmother." An old woman with white hair appeared before them.

"Like I said, that's going to take some getting used to," remarked Avery.

Although Zäria did not trust the witch, she was quite amused with her ability to change her appearance. "We should go with the grandmother."

"I can carry you both in this." Weezelbet held out a basket to the faeries.

Avery looked at the basket and then at the witch. "No, we aren't gonna walk into a trap like that. You get inside, and we'll come in through a window or something."

"Still don't trust me?"

"Don't trust anyone just yet," Avery replied. "Show us the way to the inn."

"It's right up this path." Weezelbet pointed to a worn dirt path through the woods. The faeries followed the witch-grandmother down the path until they saw a small, rickety shack. There was a broken sign crookedly hanging on the door that read Fig Cove Luxury Inn.

Avery scoffed. "Luxury Inn? You want to stay here? The tree is looking better by the second."

"When are you going to learn that looks are deceiving?" the witch-grandmother asked. "You'd better hide now. I'll open a window when I get in." The faeries waited behind a bush while the witch knocked on the door.

A few minutes later, a young woman with red hair opened the door. She looked over the old woman before her and asked, "Can I help you?"

Weezelbet replied in her sweetest grandmother voice, "I'm on my way to visit my grandchildren. It's getting late, and I need a place to rest 'til morning. Do you have any room here?"

The woman thought for a moment before she answered. "Yes, we have lots of room, but it will cost you two gold pieces."

"Two gold pieces? That seems a bit high," the witch-grandmother complained.

"Then be on your way. I will take no less." The woman started to close the door.

Weezelbet quickly said, "No. I can't go any farther tonight. If two pieces is the price to rest, then I will pay it." Weezelbet pulled two gold pieces from her coin purse and placed them in the innkeeper's hand. The woman opened the door and the witch-grandmother disappeared inside.

When the door closed, the two faeries quietly flew around the shack, looking for an open window. To Zäria's dismay, the shack appeared to have no windows. Then she noticed one of the shingles on the side of the building opened up and let light out.

Weezelbet was still in her grandmother form and signaled for the faeries to come in. "Quickly, quickly," Weezelbet whispered.

Once the faeries were in, Zäria looked around the room. It was much larger than the whole shack appeared from the outside. The walls were decorated with flowery paper. The bed was covered with plush warm blankets and pillows. There was a table set with bread, butter, and tea next to a crackling fire that warmed their chilled faces.

"Wow," Zäria exclaimed.

"You weren't kidding about looks being deceiving, but how is this possible?" Avery asked.

Weezelbet changed back into her witch form and took a seat in a chair by the bed. Then she matter-of-factly said, "This is a witch's inn."

"A witch's inn?" Avery shouted. "You took us to a coven? Why did you bother changing your form?"

"I didn't want to alarm you. And the innkeeper could tell I was in disguise; that's why she charged so much." She picked up a piece of bread from the table. "I used real gold to pay for this room, and it's definitely warmer than a tree." She took a bite of the bread. "And the food is good too—a lot better than eating a cold faerie." She grinned.

"Witches eat faeries?" Zäria asked, frightened.

Weezelbet laughed; "Witches will eat anything—eye of newt, tail of fox …" She cackled loudly. "I jest with you." She reached out her hand with some bread. "Are you hungry?"

Zäria stared at the bread for a moment and looked up at the witch. "Yes, I am hungry," she said as she took a small piece of bread from the witch's hand. She quickly took a bite. "Oh, this is delicious and warm." She put what was left in her mouth and went to the table to get more.

"Zäria, you shouldn't eat that," Avery scolded. "We don't know if it's safe."

"It's fine," Weezelbet said. "I'm eating it too, and I haven't keeled over and died."

Avery looked at Zäria, who still was enjoying her bite of bread. He took a piece, smelled it, and then took a small bite. It was warm and delicious.

Weezelbet took a small pillow off the bed, laid it on the floor near the fire, and covered it with a washcloth. "Will this work for a bed for you?"

"That will be fine for Zäria. I'll sleep in that chair over there." Avery pointed to a cushioned chair in the corner.

"Very well; here's something to use as a blanket." The witch placed a knitted scarf on the chair and lay down in the bed.

Avery and Zäria sat at the table facing the fire. Zäria whispered to Avery, "I think she's a nice witch."

"I'm not so sure. With everything that's happened, it's hard to trust anyone. Even our queen has kept important secrets from us, secrets that might cost us our lives."

"Let's get some sleep. We have a long way to go, and who knows what tomorrow brings?" Zäria snuggled up in her soft pillow bed, yawned, and fell asleep.

Avery had a challenging time letting himself sleep, even though it was so warm and comfy. Eventually, he gave in and fell asleep. He awoke to Zäria's tapping him on the arm.

"Avery, Avery. I didn't want to wake you, but it's getting late," she said.

Avery looked around, momentarily forgetting where they had spent the night. Everything looked the same, and nothing was out of the ordinary. He sat up and stretched out his wings and legs. "Where is Weezelbet? Did she ditch us here?"

"No, she's downstairs having breakfast with the innkeeper."

"There's a downstairs in this place?" He wiped the sleep from his eyes.

"She offered to bring us some food, but I made us a breakfast with our own supplies. I thought you'd like that better." She pointed up at the table.

"Thank you, Zäria."

"You're welcome. C'mon, let's eat. I waited for you to wake up, and now I'm starving." They flew up to the tabletop, where Zäria had set out nuts, berries, and sunflower seeds on a flowery plate. "I made you some sunflower tea." She poured some in two cups she'd taken from her satchel.

"This looks really good," Avery said as he picked up an almond and started to eat.

Weezelbet came back into the room as they were packing up. "Ready to go?"

"Just about," said Avery.

"Do you want me to meet you out front?" Weezelbet asked.

"That won't be necessary. You can take us in the basket," Zäria replied.

Weezelbet's eyes got big and her voice high, "Oh, you like me now, do ya?"

Avery grinned. "For a witch, you're not half bad."

"For a faerie, you're not so bad yourself."

They all laughed a bit. Avery and Zäria hid themselves in the basket, and Weezelbet carried them out of the inn. When they were out of sight, the witch opened the basket and let the faeries fly out. Weezelbet changed back into the crow, and they all set off into the air.

"How far is this forest, Weezelbet?" Avery asked.

"It will take a few days to reach it," she replied.

"That's what I was afraid of."

Zäria shivered. "Has anyone else noticed how cold it has gotten? My wings are freezing."

Suddenly aware of his surroundings, Avery said, "Yeah, it is kind of cold, now that you mention it."

"Phantom mists," Weezelbet announced, "bring a chill to your bones. It's time to stop."

"But we just started," Avery protested.

Weezelbet swooped down to land in a nearby tree. Avery and Zäria followed. Weezelbet flew to the ground and changed back into her witch form before her feet hit dirt. "If you fly any farther through the phantom mists, you will freeze to death, evaporate, and become a phantom mist," she declared.

"How do we pass them then?" Zäria asked.

"We need to keep warm. I'll have to carry you through this area."

"How will you stay warm, though?"

"I'll wear a coat." She snapped her fingers and was suddenly wrapped in a fur coat, along with a hat and gloves. She was still holding the basket she had used to carry them earlier, but it was now filled with rabbit furs. "I would have made coats for you too, but that would make it really hard for you to fly, and your wings would still freeze."

"How long do you think it will it take to get past them?" asked Avery.

"Half a day, at least," the witch replied.

"You want us to sit in that basket for half a day?" Avery asked.

"I don't want you to. You can try to fly and hope your wings don't freeze into icicles. It's up to you."

"Fine," said Avery. Then both faeries settled into the basket.

Zäria tried to assure Avery. "It is warm in here, Avery, and so soft."

The witch closed the lid, and off they went.

CHAPTER 8

Witchery

very felt like he was going to throw up. The motion inside the basket made his stomach hurt. He had a headache, and he was disoriented after spending hours in there with Zäria. "I don't think I can take much more of this," he said, groaning.

"Me either," Zäria said.

More time passed. Finally, the lid of the basket was opened. Light and frigid air touched their faces. Avery assumed it must be late afternoon now.

They were still surrounded by trees, so it looked like they hadn't traveled far at all. "Where are we?" Zäria asked, wiping her eyes.

"We are still in West Woods. I had to walk a few miles out of the way to get around the mists. They kept moving, so I had to keep changing directions."

"Do you still know which direction to go?" Avery asked.

"Give me your map, and I'll make sure I took the right path."

Zäria looked at Avery for approval, and he nodded to her. Zäria pulled the map out of a satchel and opened it up. She looked at it for a moment and then looked around at the trees.

"Give it here now," Weezelbet said impatiently, waving her hands at Zäria. The witch took the map and studied it. "Seems to be in order," Weezelbet confirmed. She rolled the map back up and looked at the faeries.

"Which way do we go, Weezelbet?" Avery asked.

"Doesn't matter," the witch replied.

"Doesn't matter? Of course it matters. What are you talking about?" Avery said angrily.

The witch smirked. "No matter which way you go, you're dead."

Avery looked at Zäria who was biting her lip.

"Phantom mists behind you, fire swamps ahead, and witches on both sides," Weezelbet said. With that, dozens of witches appeared from every direction, encircling them.

"And no map!" exclaimed a decrepit old witch with a raspy voice. She snatched the map from Weezelbet's hands.

"You tricked us!" Zäria shouted.

"I'm a witch. What did you expect?" Weezelbet cackled. "Now we can have this seed and its power for ourselves!"

The other witches hissed and emitted high-pitched laughs.

"You don't even know what it's for," Zäria said.

"That won't be hard to find out, once we have it," said the craggy witch who held the map.

The sun was dipping below the horizon, and it was getting darker by the minute. Avery flew at the witch and grabbed the map. He pulled and pulled on it, but it was no use.

The witch laughed loudly. "Ignorant faeries, don't you know anything? This map is enchanted. You have to hand it over willingly. And I'm not about to give it to you."

With that, all of the witches began to spin wildly in circles, and they disappeared in puffs of smoke. When the air cleared, the faeries were alone, stranded in the dark.

"It's entirely my fault," Zäria ashamed. "I just gave it to her. Now we're stuck here … and lost."

"It's not your fault. She made us trust her. It was all a trick. And besides, I told you to give it to her. Don't blame yourself."

"I still should have known better."

"I know. I feel that way too. She was a witch, after all. You looked at the map before you handed it to Weezelbet. Do you remember which way to go?"

"I couldn't make much sense of it because I don't know where we are to begin with. She could have taken us anywhere."

"Weezelbet said something about fire swamps ahead of us. Did you see fire swamps on the map?"

Zäria thought about it for a moment, trying to remember the map. "I'm not sure," she said, disheartened.

"It's okay, Zär." Avery wrapped an arm around her. "We'll find the way."

Zäria started to sob. "This is scarier than the dungeon, Avery. And I miss my family, and Yamani, and even caring for the garden."

"Maybe we could fly up to the canopy and see where we are."

"It's too dark to see anything right now," she replied, wiping the tears away.

"There must be an owl up there somewhere, right? They can see in the dark."

"An owl? Now you're really talking crazy, Avery. An owl would eat us."

"I'm not scared of an owl," he said, looking up into the trees.

"Well, I am."

Avery saw the look on Zäria's face. "Okay, we'll just have to wait it out until daylight then."

"Where are we going to stay? It's already getting cold."

Avery flew over to the trees and examined a couple. "Found it!" he exclaimed.

"Found what?" Zäria asked.

"I found a place to stay. This old tree is hollow. It's even big enough inside to have a fire."

Zäria flew to the hollow tree and peeked inside. "Wow, it's huge in here. This is bigger than both our houses put together."

"With a fire, we should stay warm enough for the night."

Zäria's tears were gone and replaced by a smile and a glow in her eyes. "Then we'll need to gather some kindling." With that, she quickly flew off to pick up dry pine needles and twigs. Avery started making a pile of pine cones and leaves inside the hollow of the tree. He then cleared an area in the center to build a small fire. Zäria brought in the kindling she'd gathered and quickly began stacking them in the spot Avery prepared for the fire. It didn't take long for Avery to get the fire burning with a little faerie magic.

"That should last a while." He dusted off his hands and went to make a bed for the night.

"How are we going to find that stupid seed without the map, Avery?"

"I'm not sure. We'll just have to continue in the direction we've been going and hope for the best."

"That's not very reassuring. What if the witches find it first?"

"Thordon said it had to be a faerie, so maybe they can't. We don't even know what it is. I don't have a better answer than that. Sorry."

Zäria sat quietly for a moment, warming her hands by the fire. "What was it that Yamani said to do if we were in need?" She closed her eyes and put her hands on her head, trying to remember. "Look for a tree or something ..."

"That's right." Avery perked up, piecing together the words in his mind that Yamani had said. "She said there is a sanctuary in an ancient tree."

"Let's try to find it, Avery."

"It may not be real, Zäria."

"We should try. We are lost and in need. Besides, we don't have a lot of other options here."

"All right. We'll fly up to the canopy in the morning, figure out where we are, and go from there. But for now, we should get some sleep.

The chill of the morning frost woke Avery, only to find that Zäria was already up and preparing to leave.

"We'd better get going soon," she said, "or our wings will freeze while we're sitting still."

"Right. How long have you been awake?" He looked around and saw that everything was packed, the fire was out, and she had cleaned up the area to look as if they were never there.

"Oh, I don't know—a while, I guess. I'm not making it easy for anyone to track us.

Both faeries stepped out of the cavernous tree into the sunlight and took flight. Once above the trees, they were able to determine their location a little better and decide the best route to take.

"I think we should try to track the witches," Avery said.

"Track the witches? Are you crazy?"

"No, they have the map, so if we follow them, they will lead us to where we need to go."

"That's a great plan, except how are we going to follow witches when they can look like anyone or anything they want?"

"I didn't think of that. Well, this is the direction we were headed already. We should keep going this way, and just keep our eyes open for anyone who might be a witch."

Zäria realized they must have been traveling north the entire time, based on the moss growing on the trees. She tried to remember any identifying place markers from the map, but instead she saw vivid glimpses of places she had never seen before and then a bright light. *I must be exhausted from flying for hours,* she thought. *It might be time for a break.* "Avery, I need to rest a bit."

They landed on a hillside in the shade to eat and rest. Zäria thought the place seemed peaceful enough—almost as if they weren't on a dangerous journey to find a seed that ultimately would save their lives.

They sat quietly as they ate until Zäria broke the silence. "I've been thinking about that map. I looked at it a few times, and I've been trying to remember anything I saw."

"Well? Did you remember anything?"

"Yeah, there was a picture of a stone wall. I remember it because it had purple flowers growing through it. I don't remember how far it is from where we are going, but at least it's a landmark to look for." She didn't want to tell Avery just yet that she didn't see it on the map but had had a vision of being there. She had seen little visions before but nothing so vivid and clear. She didn't want Avery to think she was losing her mind.

"That's good, Zäria. Keep trying to remember all that you can. I've been thinking we really should go in search of that tree Yamani was telling us about. But that's something else to look for. I guess we have a lot of reasons to keep our eyes open—witches, stone walls, and ancient tree faerie sanctuaries."

Zäria giggled, despite the seriousness of their dilemma. Their lighthearted moment was short-lived when a black crow flew past. Was it just a crow, or was it Weezelbet? The faeries looked at each other, and without hesitation, both took off after the crow. Zäria yelled, "Weezelbet! Is that you, you horrible lying witch?" *If I had rocks,* she thought, *I'd throw them at that crow.*

The crow, realizing it was being chased, tried to take cover by swooping down below the canopy of the trees. It was no use. The faeries were on a mission to catch up. They flew around trees, under branches, and through a thorny thicket until they lost sight of the crow.

The weary faeries landed on a tree limb high above the forest. Avery continued to look in all directions for the black crow but did not see it anywhere.

Zäria nearly collapsed as she tried to catch her breath. "It had to be Weezelbet. That bird had us flying around in circles on purpose to get us lost."

"Well she did a terrible job of it. I think I see that stone wall from the map," Avery said as he moved some leaves out of the way and pointed.

Zäria perked up and looked in the direction Avery was pointing. "Where?"

"Follow me. Let's just go down there and get a better look." Avery flew off with Zäria following closely behind. After getting past some of the taller trees, Zäria could finally see the wall too. It was just like in her vision.

"Oh, I see it now, Avery. It has the purple flowers covering it, just like the picture on the map."

It was farther away than it appeared because Zäria felt like it took an eternity to reach it. They both landed on top of the wall, looking around.

Avery asked, "Does anything else look familiar from the map, Zär? Was this wall close to the sanctuary?"

"The sanctuary wasn't on the map, so I'm not sure how close we are. This wall is really all I remember because it was at the end of the Perished Forest. I took it for granted that we would always have the map with us, so I didn't make a point to memorize it."

"Do you think we are supposed to cross the wall or follow it?"

"I'm not sure. I really wish we had somebody to ask for help."

No sooner had she finished her sentence than a bright light appeared before them, nearly blinding them both. They quickly put their hands up to shield their eyes from the glaring light.

This must be the light from my vision, Zäria thought.

She heard a small gruff voice. "What are you doing?"

Zäria put her hands down to see who was talking to them. The light was gone, but it took a moment for her eyes to adjust. Before them stood a tiny bearded gnome. He had a chubby pink face with a scraggily white beard. Zäria wanted to pinch his cheeks, but she refrained.

"Did you make that bright light?" asked Zäria.

"What bright light?" asked the gnome.

"Never mind." *I wonder if the light was just part of my vision, and I'm the only one who saw it.*

"You faeries ought to get inside the sanctuary. This forest isn't safe." He gestured behind him to a tree.

Zäria and Avery both turned their attention in the direction the gnome was pointing. There stood an enormous tree, twisting dramatically up from the roots that clutched the earth and decorated with patches of green moss and fanned fungi. Branches with swaying leaves protruded wildly from the top in a tangled mess. Wisteria had tangled its vines throughout the tree, giving off a sweet scent from its scattered lavender flowers. Zäria stood in awe of the majestic sight. It was the most gorgeous tree she had ever seen.

"How did we not see this before?" asked Avery, staring at the tree.

"It's so beautiful," Zäria cooed.

"Yes, yes, very beautiful and magical. Follow me," said the gnome dismissively as he waddled along toward the tree.

Zäria did not notice a door or entrance of any kind, but the gnome touched a tree root, and it lifted up, forming a doorway. He motioned for the faeries to enter. Once inside, the doorway closed with the gnome behind them.

Inside was almost as blinding as the light Zäria had seen outside. Everything sparkled, as if drenched in glitter and diamonds. The faeries that fluttered by were the most beautiful she'd ever seen, and they too appeared to sparkle.

The gnome walked in front of them. "Come this way. This is the oldest living faerie sanctuary, Ellyngshyme."

"Living?" Avery repeated.

The gnome ignored Avery and kept walking. "My name is Oggbotham. Everyone calls me Ogg."

They followed him through a corridor and down sparkling quartz steps. When they reached the landing, Avery saw three different options: another stairway leading up, a long passageway straight ahead, and a closed door to their right. Ogg continued straight through the passageway, which was lit by fireflies. Zäria admired how their glowing light danced across the glittering walls. The long corridor opened into a cavernous room filled with faeries, elves, and several other creatures.

"Wow, you all live here together?" asked Zäria. She had seen fae only in her village.

"Yes," replied Ogg, "but some are only visiting."

"I thought this was a *faerie* sanctuary," Avery said.

"It is, but King Byron doesn't believe in turning away anyone in need," Ogg explained.

They crossed the bustling room to a large double door with guards on either side. Ogg muttered something to one of the guards while pointing toward the faeries behind him. The guards shuffled to open the doors. As the doors opened, the room behind them became unsettlingly quiet. Zäria realized every creature had stopped what they were doing to stare at them.

Ogg turned around with his hand in the air to address the curious crowd. "No need to fret, friends. Carry on. Go, go, go."

Slowly the room filled with whispers and then loud chatter until it was bustling again. Ogg motioned to the faeries to enter the throne room. He nodded to the guards to close the doors behind them. Once the doors were closed, the only sounds Zäria heard were trickling water in the fountains beside the throne and music from a golden harp-like instrument that a small faerie was playing at the far end of the room.

A guard entered the room from behind the throne. Zäria guessed he was an elf—he didn't have wings but was dressed in faerie armor. He also didn't sparkle like everything else in Ellyngshyme, but he did have a radiant glow about him. He spoke in a melodic tone when he announced the king. "The omniscient King Byron approaches. Bow and show your respect."

Ogg knelt on bended knee. The faeries followed suit. The guard took a couple of steps back and knelt on bended knee as well. King Byron entered the room with his faeries-in-waiting tending to his royal robes. Zäria was mesmerized by how wise and powerful he appeared. He was faerish, with large, iridescent, glittering green wings. His robes were a rich violet and swept the floor as he appeared to glide to his throne with only the slightest movement of his wings. He had flowing, shining white hair that matched his snow-white beard. He took a seat on his throne and nodded to the guard as the faeries-in-waiting strategically placed the king's robes at his feet and then took their places encircling the throne.

"Ogg, it appears you have brought us some guests. Who might these young faeries be?" The king's voice was so warm and welcoming that Zäria instantly felt safe when she heard him speak.

"Good King Byron, these faeries came to Ellyngshyme in need. They are Avery and Zäria." Ogg gestured to the fae kneeling beside him.

"In need?" the king asked. "Well, this is, in fact, a sanctuary." He smiled at the faeries. "How can I help you?"

Avery took a deep breath and said, "Thordon has sent us on a quest for a seed in exchange for our lives. A witch tricked us and took our map. We are not sure what this seed is that we are looking for, and now without the map, we are a bit lost, Your Majesty."

King Byron seemed interested in the story. "You say you are looking for a seed, but you don't know what kind?"

"Yes, Your Majesty," replied Avery. "We only know it's in the Perilous Forest."

The king stroked his long white beard. "Hmm. The only seeds that I'm aware of being recovered from the Perilous Forest were from the giant cocoa bean plant. We have been trying to make them grow but have failed miserably. If we could get them to grow, it would come in handy for its great healing abilities. There is only one left untouched. Do you think this might be the seed you search for? A cocoa plant seems hardly worth risking lives over."

"It may very well be the seed Thordon wants," Zäria answered. "He has been making a lot of chocolate confections and has a chocolate-eating dragon. He said only a faerie could retrieve the seed. If he knew it was here, that would make sense."

"Did you say a chocolate-eating dragon?"

"Yes, I did." Zäria was worried that she might have said too much.

"Eguin," the king said. "Why on earth does Thordon need the dwarfs' dragon?" He seemed to be asking himself more than the faeries. He became lost in thought as he seemed to run possible answers to that question in his head. Then he turned his attention to Ogg and the faeries. "Ogg, I will require the royal messengers and advisers immediately."

"Of course, Your Majesty." Ogg bowed.

"And please make accommodations for the young fae. Provide them with food and drink and any other supplies they require." King Byron smiled at Avery and Zäria. "I hope we can make you comfortable during your stay. We will discuss this further in the morning, after you've rested."

The king stood up from his throne and proceeded to leave the room. His faeries-in-waiting quickly gathered up his robes and followed him. The guard escorted the fae and Ogg out of the throne room.

After crossing through the busy cavern and several winding passageways, they arrived at their rooms. Avery was relieved his room was across the hall from Zäria's. The door on the left had golden swirling letters that read "Damsel 42" and the door to the right read "Gent 43."

The guard opened the door to Damsel 42 and stepped back into the hall. Ogg entered the room and motioned to Zäria to follow. "Come along, then," he said.

Zäria shrugged at Avery and followed Ogg into the room.

The guard then opened the door to Gent 43 and escorted Avery into the room. "Everything in good order?" the guard asked him.

"Yes, very much so. Thank you," replied Avery.

"Supper will be brought to you shortly, and someone will fetch you both in the morning to breakfast with King Byron."

"Right, of course," Avery said absentmindedly. He was busy taking in the room. It was bigger than his entire house. In the far right corner stood a four-poster bed, which looked to be made of wisteria branches. The canopy was draped with an emerald-green fabric unlike anything he had seen before. A small table with two chairs were in the middle of the room; a small plate of acorns was on the table. He turned around when he heard Zäria come in behind him.

"Can you believe these rooms?" she asked excitedly. "They are so big. How could they even fit in this place?"

"Must be faerie magic," Avery replied. "What does your room look like?"

Zäria grabbed Avery's arm. "Come look!"

When he reached the doorway, Avery saw her bed was identical to his, except with violet bedding instead of green. Even though they were underground, her room had two large stained-glass windows that let in a glowing light. "They sure like to show off their faerie magic here," said Avery.

"Maybe they are just trying to make us comfortable, Avery."

"Well, it's definitely nicer than Thordon's place." Avery laughed, but Zäria shuddered.

"Don't even joke about that place," she said.

"Oh, there you are," called a cheerful voice behind them. They both turned to see a gnome woman carrying a wooden tray. She ambled over to the table, set the tray down, and started setting everything out. Without looking up, she said, "I'm sure you two are hungry. I've brought you some poppy cake. I baked it fresh this morning. And some honeyed dandelion milk. That ought to keep you 'til morn, I s'pose." She wiped her hands on her apron and stepped back.

Zäria and Avery took a seat at the table. Avery was very hungry and glad to have more than nuts and berries for a meal. "Thank you so much. It looks delicious," he said to the woman.

The gnome woman smiled. "I hope you'll enjoy it. My name is Fynn. If you need anything at all, just ring the little bell next to each of your beds. I bid you good night."

"Good night," they said in unison.

Fynn left them to their supper.

"I really like it here," Zäria said as she poured a cup of milk.

Avery took a bite of poppy cake. "I hope King Byron will help us. It's nice here, but I would like to return home."

"So would I, Avery. I'm tired. I think we should get some sleep while we are in a safe place."

"You're right." Avery finished his last bite of cake and drank his dandelion milk. He hugged Zäria good night before he left the room and closed the door behind him.

Back in his own room, Avery flopped on his bed without bothering to pull the covers back. He was asleep almost before his head hit the pillow.

CHAPTER 9

Breakfast

Avery tossed and turned as he kept hearing the ringing of a bell. He finally opened his eyes and realized the ringing wasn't a dream but rather the tiny bell next to his bed. He reached over and grabbed the bell to hold it still. "Okay, okay, I'm awake." The bell silenced.

Avery made his way to the door and opened it to find Ogg standing there. The gnome did not look happy that he'd been kept waiting. "Took you long enough. It's time for breakfast. King Byron is not as patient as I," he said gruffly.

"Why didn't you just come in and wake me?" Avery asked.

"Can't. Door was closed," Ogg said. "The doors are charmed to only be opened by permission of the occupant."

"From now on, Ogg, you have my permission to open the door to any room I'm in." Avery splashed some morning dew on his face and stretched out his arms and wings. "I'm as ready as I'll ever be. Let's go."

On the way out the door, Ogg said, "Fynn escorted your friend Zäria to the feast hall while I was waiting on you." They continued down the hall and through a few corridors before arriving at the feast hall.

It was a large room with lofty ceilings. Candles lined the walls and were on the center of each table. There were five long tables in the room, but only one was set with food and tableware. Avery saw Zäria, Fynn, and King Byron sitting at the far end, along with another fae, a dwarf, and two elves.

King Byron looked up from his conversation with the fae sitting to his left. "Avery. Good of you to join us. Breakfast has just been brought to the table. Please sit."

Avery took the open seat next to Zäria. "My apologies, King Byron. I fear your beds here are far too comfortable for waking early," Avery said with a smile.

King Byron chuckled a bit. "Well, I'll see to switching your bed with a briar patch next time."

Everyone laughed. Zäria, however, did not find Avery's tardiness very funny. She nudged his arm and then addressed the king. "Thank you so much for allowing us to stay here, Your Majesty."

"It is my pleasure. This is a faerie sanctuary, after all; is it not?" The king addressed Avery. "You missed introductions. This"—he gestured to the fae—"is my oldest friend and royal adviser, Goran."

"Good to know you," said Goran to Avery.

The king continued introductions, gesturing to the others at the table. "Rorik is my most faithful of dwarf guards." Rorik smirked and only nodded at Avery. "And of course, the very talented twins, Fern and Franz. If you are ever in need of any type of gadget or anything to be manufactured, they will undoubtedly surpass your expectations."

The twins looked at each other and quietly giggled at the compliment.

"It is a magnificent pleasure to meet all of you," said Avery as he started loading up his plate with food.

"Now that you are both here," Goran said, "I wanted to ask some questions about your state of affairs." When the two faeries nodded and continued eating their breakfast, he said, "What does Thordon have planned for this seed that is so important he sent you on a treacherous quest to fetch it?"

"We don't know," Avery said, "but we believe it has something to do with Eguin. That's Thordon's dragon."

"Eguin is most definitely *not* Thordon's dragon," Rorik said angrily in a gruff voice.

"Rorik, the fae meant nothing by it. He simply doesn't know the dragon's history with us," the king said. Avery was embarrassed by this faux pas, but King Byron reassured him. "It's quite all right, young fae. Please continue."

Avery looked at Zäria; she nodded to him. "His Majesty is correct; we really don't know anything about the dragon. We snuck into Eerie Hollow and found elves creating many different chocolate confections with huge vats of chocolate. We didn't know until after Thordon captured us that he had a chocolate-eating dragon, which he called Eguin. Even after our queen, Yamani, came to claim us, Thordon refused to set us free unless we completed the task of delivering this seed to him."

"You agreed to this?" asked Goran.

"We didn't have much of a choice. It is our only way to return home and ensure the safety of our people," Zäria said.

"Or it is the absolute end of your people? Did it ever occur to you that Thordon is plotting a weapon for attack?" Rorik asked.

"Honestly, our only concern was our freedom," Avery said sadly, feeling selfish at that moment.

King Byron announced, "I want to see this seed that has become so important. Ogg, have the seed brought to our table immediately."

"Right away, sire." Ogg left the room and returned within minutes. Avery thought he had returned without the seed until Ogg opened his stubby hand to reveal a tiny brown seed. Ogg laid it on the table in front of King Byron.

Avery stared at the seed with disappointment. This was what they were risking their wings over? How could this seed turn into anything important?

King Byron turned to his adviser. "Goran, what do you make of this?"

Goran sighed and shook his head. "I'm surprised this tiny seed has caused such an uproar, but it does appear that the sanctuary is the only thing preventing Thordon from obtaining this seed, and the fae have been pawns played in a game."

The king then turned to Rorik. "You were the dragon-keeper during the time Eguin dwelled in our sanctuary. Perhaps you can shed some light on this."

Rorik's face had the twisted look of regret as he spoke. "Eguin can be as dangerous as any dragon, when provoked. Chocolate makes him stronger. It increases his magic. If Thordon has been feeding him the amount of chocolate these fae say he is making, there may not be any match to Eguin's capabilities." He asked the faeries, "Where was the dragon kept?"

"In a cave in Eerie Hollow," Zäria replied.

"Thordon is a fool, and it will play to our advantage. Building up a dragon's strength is fruitless if you do not allow him to fly and train. Thordon is merely creating a fat, lazy, albeit magical dragon. Unless it's only the magic he is after."

A small voice chimed in. "That makes sense." It was Franz. "If Thordon is building up Eguin's magic, making him slow and fat could be the way of controlling the dragon."

Goran gasped. "Thordon is planning something requiring a lot of magical power. Whatever that may be, it can't be good."

"I agree, Goran. Perhaps we need to prepare ourselves," King Byron said.

"We won't allow the fae to bring the seed to Thordon, will we? That's just handing him the weapon he wants," Rorik exclaimed, clearly appalled.

"Yes, we will, and you are going with them; we all are," the king said matter-of-factly. Everyone at the table was taken aback.

"If I may be so bold," Goran said, "may I ask why, Your Majesty?"

"It does seem like a harmless cocoa seed," the king said, "and if our faeries couldn't get it to grow with our faerie magic, what is Thordon going to accomplish? I feel it is our duty to escort Avery and Zäria out of the Perilous Forest and return them safely to Saizia."

"I fear we may be underestimating Thordon's ability, sire, but I will respect your wishes," Goran said.

The king nodded. "Rorik, gather up a troop of your best guards. Goran, I trust that you will be able to provide guidance and report back to me as needed." Goran nodded in response. "Take along anyone you feel will offer the magical assistance we may require. Before we depart, strengthen the protections on the sanctuary. I don't want Thordon to think he's leaving us vulnerable in any way."

"Yes, Your Majesty. I'll start right away," Goran said.

"Franz and Fern, I want you to accompany us to aid when needed. Gather supplies and tools for the journey." Both elves nodded eagerly.

Rorik asked the king, "When shall we depart, Your Majesty?"

"We'll set out as soon as you have gathered your troops and supplies, of course. No time to be wasted. Make haste. I will leave you to your work. Advise me when you are ready."

With that, King Byron stood and left the room, with his entourage following close behind.

"Well, you heard the king's orders," Goran barked. "No time to waste. Meet in the throne room once everyone has prepared."

Avery escorted Zäria to her room to gather her belongings. Once all her things were packed, they moved on to Avery's room. They heard the bell ring, signaling that someone was at the door. Avery opened the door to find Fynn waiting with a large bag. "Would you like to come in?" he asked.

"Oh no," she said. "I just brought you some provisions for your long trip. I can't have you going hungry." She handed the bag to Avery. "There are some warm muffins, nuts, and berries I picked this morn. Plenty of dandelion milk and honey."

"Thank you so much, Fynn," said Zäria. "You didn't have to go to so much trouble, but we really appreciate it."

"It's no trouble at all. Franz and Fern have asked for you to come down to the cellars." Seeing a look of concern on Zäria's face, she added, "That's where they keep all their contraptions. I'll show you the way. It's easy to get lost in the sanctuary corridors."

They followed Fynn through the passageways, past the throne room and down a steep, winding stone staircase. It got darker as they descended, despite the lit torches along the walls.

Avery could hear the faint sound of clanking metal and voices ahead. The sound grew louder the farther they went. A light shone through the open door at the end of the corridor. Fynn walked in. "I brought the young fae, as you asked, Franz. Stop by the kitchen before your journey. I have some blueberry acorn cookies cooling for you."

"Thanks, Fynn. Those are my favorite," said Franz.

"I know. Good luck to you all. I must get back to the kitchen. Lots to do." With that, she made her way back to the main level.

Franz motioned for Zäria and Avery to come in. "Fern and I wanted to show you some of our inventions."

Fern nodded but continued working on the metal gadget on the table in front of her. Franz pointed at a very large contraption that stood in the middle of the room and almost touched the ceiling. It was made of wood, grapevines, and what appeared to be bones. Metal discs spun in different directions and pulled the grapevines around and through the contraption in a rhythmic fashion. It was the craziest thing Avery had ever seen.

"This is Margolotte," Franz said.

"Margolotte? Are those bones?" Zäria asked, confused.

"Yes, Margolotte. She was an amazing horse, but she died, so we used her bones to make this horse-powered bang-along," Fern explained.

Avery asked, "What exactly is a bang-along?"

"Oh, it does all sorts of useful things. You can sleep on it, ride it through the garden, dig holes, and cook on it. Whatever you need," Franz said. "We want to take this one with us."

"That thing is huge. How do you plan on getting it out of the sanctuary?" asked Zäria.

"In my pocket," he said.

Zäria laughed. "You must have pretty big pockets, Franz."

"Oh, I will shrink it, of course. We have plenty of shrink powder."

"I bet that comes in handy," said Avery.

"It does." Franz directed their attention to a cauldron over the fire. "That is another batch brewing. It's almost done."

Fern packed away the metal gadget that she'd been working on and walked over to the cauldron. As she reached out her hand to grab it off the fire, Avery was about to shout, "Stop, it's hot," but just before Fern touched the cauldron, the fire died out, and the cauldron disappeared. A bowl appeared in Fern's hands that was full of a purplish powder.

"Magic never ceases to amaze me," Avery said.

Franz laughed. "If given the right amount of effort, there are no limits to its power."

"I am beginning to understand that."

Fern packed some of the powder into a leather bag and poured the rest into a large wooden vase and set it up on a shelf. She then tied the bag to her belt. "I think we have everything ready to go unless Avery and Zäria can think of anything else useful we should bring." She looked at them both, but they just shrugged.

"It's hard to know what we might need. We are still very new to this," said Avery.

"Very well then. Fern and I are ready to go," said Franz

Together, they made their way through the corridors and up to the throne room to meet with the others.

CHAPTER 10

Preparations

When Zäria, Avery, and the twins arrived at the throne room, Rorik and three other guards were already there. Zäria thought two of the guards looked much younger than Rorik but very strong. The third looked like he had seen his share of war. Rorik and his group were packing up gear.

"Here's the fae now, Avery and Zäria," Rorik said. "We will need to make sure they make it to Eerie Hollow unharmed, with the seed intact."

One of the younger guards asked, "So we're babysitting fae instead of protecting the sanctuary?"

Rude, Zäria thought, *and uncalled for*!

Rorik stepped forward, but the other older guard quickly stepped in front of him and spoke to the young dwarf in a gruff tone. "No, Baro, babysitting is what I'm doing, bringing you two along. I expect you both to act like royal guards of Ellyngshyme at all times. Do you understand?"

The two guards suddenly stood up straighter, and Baro said, "Yes, Drovak, I understand completely."

Drovak then turned to Avery and Zäria. "I'm sorry, young fae. Baro and Korgan are still learning the ways of the Royal Guard and forgot their places for a moment. I am Drovak. Rorik and I have fought and won many battles together. I assure you that you will be well protected on our journey out of the Perilous Forest and back to Saizia with the cocoa seed."

"Thank you," Avery said nervously, not really knowing what else to say to this.

Drovak chuckled in response.

"Drovak, are you trying to scare the wits out of the young fae?" said Goran, just entering the room.

"Of course not, Goran. Wits are your area of expertise, are they not?"

"Especially when in your company, Drovak."

"Touché."

"Avery and Zäria," Goran said, "I would like you to meet my mother, Ambrosia."

Zäria looked at the woman next to Goran. She was very beautiful and didn't look nearly old enough to be anyone's mother, although she did have long sparkling silver hair.

Goran continued, "She has the most powerful magic I have ever seen. We just finished strengthening the wards on the sanctuary."

"Very pleased to meet you, Ambrosia," said Zäria. When she touched Ambrosia's hand, suddenly Zäria had a vision of meeting Ambrosia before. "Do I know you?"

Ambrosia smiled at the faerie. "How would I know who you know, dear? That is simply a silly question."

"I suppose you're right. You just seem so familiar to me."

Just then King Byron entered the room, along with someone who appeared to be his queen and two pixies. Everyone turned in his direction as he spoke. "Good; everyone is here. I hope you are all prepared for your journey."

"Yes, Your Majesty. It appears everything is in order here," replied Goran.

"Splendid. In discussing the matter with my dear wife, Queen Xandria, she requested that Ambrosia carry the seed for safekeeping."

The queen came forward. Zäria thought she was so lovely, dressed in an iridescent blue gown of spun silk that fluttered as she moved. Her hair was rolled into red curls and pinned with baby's breath and hydrangea flowers. She reached out and held Ambrosia's hands in hers. "Oh, Ambrosia, I am so glad you will be coming with us."

Ambrosia curtsied to the queen and replied, "Of course, Your Majesty. I wouldn't miss a chance to visit Saizia. It is wonderful here, but I do miss it now and again."

"I do know what you mean, Ambrosia. It has been far too long."

"Yes, indeed, Your Majesty."

The queen let go of Ambrosia's hands and placed a small golden satchel in them. She then turned to the king. "I am eager to leave, Byron, dear."

The king turned to the court. "Ogg, open the gate, and we will make way."

Ogg scuttled out of the room to the gate, followed by Rorik and Boro. Once outside, the two guards signaled it was safe for the king and queen to exit the sanctuary gate. Drovak and Korgan followed close behind, and then the others joined them. Ogg bid them adieu and closed the gate behind him—and it disappeared completely into the tree once again.

Zäria watched curiously as Ambrosia reached into the red satchel hanging from her waist and brought out three shiny pebbles. She then pulled a couple of branches off a nearby hawthorn bush and some wisteria blossoms from the sanctuary tree. She set them all in the king and queen's hands and waved her hand over the top while whispering a chant. She then transferred the bundle to the ground a few feet in front of them. She chanted a few more words and then sprinkled a red powder over it. A minute later there was a beautiful carriage before them, just large enough for the king and queen to ride in it.

Zäria asked Ambrosia, "What will pull the carriage?"

"Magic," exclaimed Ambrosia.

As soon as the king and queen sat down inside, the carriage rolled forward at a steady pace. The troop moved along with them, the guards walking alongside the carriage and the fae flying above. Franz and Fern trailed along behind, quietly discussing their inventions and contraptions that might be of use to them.

They made their way quickly through the woods. To Zäria, it felt so much safer traveling with their group than when she and Avery were on their own. She also noticed that the group never needed to refer to a map; they just knew the way, as if they'd been there before.

The sun was beginning to set, so the guards called the troop to a halt and got to work setting up camp. After the king and queen dismounted from the carriage, Zäria was amazed to see it quickly reverted into the pile of effects from which it had been made. Ambrosia collected the items and tucked them safely into her red satchel. Goran placed his hand on the bark of a large tree. A bright glowing light started at his hand and grew larger and larger until it was the size of a doorway. When Goran removed his hand, there was an opening in the tree that gave way to a cavernous room. He gestured inside and said, "It will be much more comfortable in here for the night."

Zäria thought of the night she'd spent inside a tree with Avery, with only a small fire for warmth. This room was full of faerie magic because it was fully furnished with beds, chairs, and tables, much like those in the sanctuary. She really wished she had her own faerie magic, but it hadn't revealed itself yet.

Come morning, Zäria was well rested and ready to continue. Franz and Fern helped her prepare breakfast with their bang-along contraption—it was made to do just about anything. While the elves and Zäria cleaned up and packed away the bang-along, Goran and Ambrosia went straight to work, opening the doorway, ridding the tree of the magical furnishings, and then enchanting the carriage for the king and queen.

They set off once again on their journey in the early morning light. The Perilous Forest was still waiting for the sun to warm up and dry the dew from the leaves and grass. The birds were waking up and cheerily singing in the trees. Zäria was admiring all their beauty when she noticed a lone black bird in a far-off tree, quietly sitting and watching them. When the bird took flight, Zäria lost sight of the it. "Avery, did you see that?"

"See what?"

"That bird over there." Zäria pointed up at a nearby tree.

"The red one?" Avery asked, squinting up at the trees ahead.

"No, there was a black bird perched in that oak tree over there, just watching us."

"You don't think it was Weezelbet, do you?"

"It did seem awfully strange, sitting there all quiet and not singing like the other birds."

"We'd better let King Byron know."

Avery and Zäria quickly flew down to the carriage window. The king noticed the young fae and said, "Oh, Avery, I do think we're making good time. Everything in order?"

"Actually, Your Majesty, Zäria just spotted an odd blackbird up ahead and fears it might be that old witch Weezelbet spying on us," said Avery.

The queen quickly leaned forward. "Did you say Weezelbet?"

"Yes. Does Your Majesty know this name?" asked Zäria.

"I surely do." The queen leaned toward the window on the other side of the carriage and shouted, "Ambrosia! I have just been informed we are perhaps being watched by the witch Weezelbet in her shape-shifted form. We need to prepare for an encounter with the coven."

Zäria almost ran into the carriage when it suddenly came to a stop, and Ambrosia cursed, "That no-good, horrible, waste-of-magic Weezelbet, up to her tricks again, no doubt. Rorik, we need to prep your guards for a coven attack. Stop here."

The guards stopped and lined up side by side. Ambrosia tapped them one by one on the shoulder, chanting all the while. Goran followed behind, repeating what Ambrosia had just done but also brushing their armor with a branch of sage. When they were finished enchanting the guards' armor, Ambrosia called to the elves. "Franz, bring out all the contraptions you brought with you. I will dust them with a little bit of witch-fighting magic."

The elves emptied their pockets and satchels, even pulling out the bang-along, and laid their belongings out in front of the fae sorceress. Ambrosia removed the cork from a small vial that was hanging around her neck. She then applied a small amount of the contents to each of the elves' inventions.

"That's all?" asked Fern.

"That's enough," replied Ambrosia. "Let's carry on, then."

Franz and Fern quickly repacked their inventions. Everyone started back on their way. The group walked on in silence, a bit more cautiously than before. Rorik and his men kept a closer watch above them, looking for witches. Ambrosia chanted quietly to herself in a rhythm that almost sounded like singing.

A gust of wind rustled the leaves around them and put everyone on edge.

Ambrosia suddenly shouted at a tree up ahead. "Weezelbet! I know it's you! I would know you in any form."

Zäria looked up and saw a familiar black bird perched on a branch. The bird spread its wings, and a swirl of blue-gray smoke encircled the bird, which quickly turned into the witch they knew as Weezelbet. She snapped her fingers, and a rickety broom appeared in her hand. The witch flew down to the group, landing directly in front of Ambrosia.

"Oh, Ambrosia, it has been ages since I've seen you make an appearance in the Perilous Forest. I hope it is your last."

"I wouldn't get your hopes up too high, Weezelbet. Where is the rest of your dirty coven?" Ambrosia looked around.

"Not far. We have been watching you. Where are you going that requires guards and magic?"

"That is none of your concern, old witch."

Weezelbet looked the guards up and down as she walked around the carriage. She walked right up to Zäria and said, "Where's the real map? You slipped me a fake, you sneaky faeries."

Zäria looked at Avery and then at Weezelbet. "You took the only map we had. I don't know what you are talking about."

"Lies!" the witch screamed. "Then how did you find the sanctuary?"

Queen Xandria had stepped down from the carriage. "The sanctuary guides faeries in need to its door. They did not need the map."

The witch whirled around to face the queen and snarled, "That map just led my coven in circles." Weezelbet looked over the troop.

"No matter. I can just make one of you take me there." She quickly grabbed the queen by the arm and pulled her close. A red glowing rope of light wrapped around Queen Xandria and held her tight.

Drovak swung his blade at the witch's magical rope and sliced right through it. The rope disappeared, and Rorik pulled the queen clear. King Byron helped the queen into the carriage, and Ambrosia put a protective magical shield around it.

"Blast you, Ambrosia!" screamed Weezelbet as she raised her hands to send a spell at the fae sorceress. But Ambrosia swiftly turned around and sent a counter-spell back at Weezelbet, knocking the witch to the ground.

Korgan thrust his sword deep into the witch's chest, pinning her where she lay. Goran threw a dark-green powder over her, and the already old witch aged before their eyes until she crinkled up, turned to dust, and was blown away with the wind. Weezelbet was gone.

Suddenly more witches appeared over Zäria's head, flying at the group from every direction. Drovak and Korgan swung their blades left and right. Boro and Rorik closely guarded the king and queen, swords drawn at the ready.

Franz and Fern took out a contraption much like a slingshot and began hurling rocks at the witches. Drovak's sword made contact with a flying witch, taking off her leg. Goran threw the green powder at the witch, and Ambrosia threw powder at the leg. She turned to ash in mid-flight. The witches were stunned momentarily by the rocks the elves were pelting at them, but it did not deter them until one hit a witch square in the eye. She lost balance and plummeted to the ground next to Boro, who swiftly impaled her with his sword.

The three remaining witches flew in circles around them. Ambrosia and Goran clasped hands and began to chant. Partway through their chant, the witches froze in their places. Everyone stood staring at the witches above them, as if in shock.

Realizing the faerie magic would hold them for only so long, Zäria grabbed a blade from the twins, flew up to the nearest witch, and lashed at her. A tingling feeling rose up from her toes, went up her arms, and shot out her fingertips. She dropped the sword in surprise. The witch broke free of the spell and fell onto Rorik's raised sword.

Zäria looked over to Avery, who was busy fighting off a witch on his own. No one seemed to be looking, so Zäria decided to see if she could recreate the zap of power she'd just felt. Since she didn't have a sword, she just threw out a punch as hard as she could. She felt that surge of power again, this time stronger. An invisible force coming from her hands appeared to have flung the last witch off her broom. The witch hovered for a few seconds instead of falling. Zäria pulled her hands back, and the witch dropped to the ground with a splat. The witch dissipated into the wind like the others.

Finally, all the witches were eradicated. Zäria landed next to Avery. She was perplexed and a little scared of this newfound power. She wanted to tell Avery but wasn't sure if she should. She decided to wait until they were alone.

Zäria noticed how exhausted Ambrosia was. "Will you be all right to continue, Ambrosia?" she asked.

The sorceress brushed off her dress and replied, "I will be fine after I have a drink of dandelion tea."

Fern brought out the bang-along and made tea, which everyone quickly drank. When they'd finished King Byron said, "We must move on. That was not the last of the coven. More dangers could await us."

"Quite right," agreed Goran.

CHAPTER 11

The Return

Avery noticed a worried look on Zäria's face. "Are you okay, Zäria?"

"Oh yeah. Something about Ambrosia is still oddly familiar." She paused and then continued. "I guess I'm just anxious about meeting with Thordon too."

"At least we don't have to face him alone," he said, gesturing to their traveling companions.

"Yes, I'm glad of it. I think we are getting close. Everything is starting to look a bit more familiar to me now."

Avery looked around more closely. He hadn't really been paying attention while talking to Zäria. They must have left the Perilous Forest a couple of miles back. Up ahead, he could see a pond full of lily pads. Then he saw King Hubert's cricket guards at the door of Ribbit Rock.

"You're right, Zäria. Look—there's Ribbit Rock." He pointed down at the pond. Then he noticed that the carriage had stopped below them. "We better go see what happened." He and Zäria landed on the ground.

"Nothing to worry about, young fae," Drovak assured them. "Queen Xandria requested we stop here for a moment." He turned to the queen and asked, "What are your orders, my queen?"

Queen Xandria said, "I wish to speak to you and Rorik privately, please."

Both guards approached the queen's side of the carriage. They spoke in tones much too quiet to hear.

"I wonder what the big secret is over there," Avery said.

"I've been thinking it was unnecessary for the king and queen to come along with us. There must be something more to why they came with us," said Zäria.

"I hadn't given that much thought to why they wanted to escort us to Saizia," Avery said, "but now that you mention it, it *does* seem odd. Still, nothing could surprise me after all we've seen."

Rorik suddenly announced, "Per the queen's request, Drovak will be heading to Saizia to fetch Queen Yamani and escort her to meet us in Erie Hollow."

That's a relief, Avery thought. *I hope it means we're going home with her this time.* He reached out for Zäria's hand. She was trembling. "I think we will be home soon, Zär," he whispered, and he held her close to calm her.

Drovak set off into the forest of Saizia with his shield and sword in hand.

Queen Yamani was in her library, reading an old journal, when Poppy came in. "Your Majesty, I've been sent to inform you that someone is approaching the kingdom. It appears to be a guard."

"Thank you, Poppy," the queen said, setting her journal on the table. "Send for my guards to escort me to the palace gate. I want to see who this visitor is."

Poppy quickly left the room and returned momentarily with three guards. Queen Yamani had placed her crown upon her head and wrapped herself in a deep-red cloak made of rose petals. Poppy curtsied to the queen and said, "I brought the guards as quickly as I could, Your Majesty"

"Yes, thank you, Poppy dear." She then addressed the guards. "How near is our visitor now?"

The guard with a curly blond beard replied, "He is almost to the gate, traveling alone. He appears to be a royal guard but not one of ours."

"Interesting. Let's head out to greet him properly, shall we?" She made her way for the door, and the guards escorted her to the gate.

A few curious fae had gathered along the path to see what news the new visitor was bringing. Yamani watched as the royal guard approached the gate. She couldn't quite see his face, but she overheard him say something to her guard about Ellyngshyme.

Queen Yamani leaned out the palace door, trying to get a better look at this guard. "I need to move closer to the gate. If he truly is delivering a message from Ellyngshyme, he can do us no harm." The guards led the queen through the palace door and down the steps to the gate. As they got closer, Yamani was able to glimpse the guard's face. "Drovak," she said aloud, relieved to recognize her visitor.

Yamani quickly headed for the gate; the guards moved in behind her, trying to keep up. She hollered at the gate guards, "Open the gate! Let him through!"

The guards opened the gate, allowing Drovak to approach the queen. He dropped to a knee and bowed before her. "Your Majesty."

"Drovak, it's been so many years since I have seen you. Please tell me that my faeries made it to Ellyngshyme safely. I cannot bear to have any more disheartening news."

Drovak stood up to address the queen. "If Avery and Zäria are the faeries you speak of, then yes, they are safe."

Yamani let out a sigh of relief. "Have you brought them with you?" the queen asked, looking past Drovak's shoulder to see if he had left them at the gate.

"Regretfully, I did not, Your Majesty. Queen Xandria sent me to request your presence. The king and queen of Ellyngshyme are waiting just outside Saizia to meet with you."

Yamani took a step back in surprise, and her welcoming smiled changed to a scowl. "The king and the queen are here and want to see me? Why did they not enter the kingdom and meet with me in the palace?"

"I do not know the answer. I only know that the queen made the importance of your presence very clear. You may bring your own guards and any necessary attendants. Our journey will not end at the meeting with the king and queen, Your Highness."

"Where are they planning on venturing?"

"I do believe that would be better answered by Her Majesty Queen Xandria, Your Highness."

"Very well, Drovak." She turned to her attendant. "Poppy, please gather what is needed for a journey and prepare to leave immediately. I will require two guards to accompany me, and those who remain at the palace should stand guard surrounding the kingdom for as long as I am absent."

One of the guards quickly left to gather all troops to follow the queen's orders.

Poppy returned with her satchels. "I am prepared to leave when you are ready, Your Majesty." She bowed her head and curtsied to the queen.

Queen Yamani signaled to her guards and said, "Very well. Let's leave at once."

The queen and her small entourage exited the palace gates, following Drovak out of Saizia.

The group had grown a tad restless while waiting for Drovak to return with Queen Yamani. The twins were busy tinkering with new inventions. The guards were sparring with their swords. Zäria and Avery decided to fly up to the canopy to flex their wings and get a glimpse of the road ahead.

Avery pointed off in the distance. "Look, there's Queen Yamani."

Zäria let go of the branch she was leaning against and turned to get a better look. "I had forgotten just how beautiful Her Majesty is."

"That she is," said a voice behind them. Zäria quickly turned to find Queen Xandria. "Come along, young fae. We have much to do."

Zäria and Avery followed the queen back down to the carriage and waited for Queen Yamani to arrive with the rest of the group. Zäria was relieved when Drovak and Yamani reached them, but she stood back to allow the king and queen of Ellyngshyme to receive them.

Queen Yamani spoke first. "Your Majesties, you sent for me?"

"Quite right," replied King Byron.

"To what do I owe the pleasure of this unexpected meeting?" inquired Yamani in a slightly sarcastic tone.

Queen Xandria sighed. "Oh, Yamani, I know it's been too long since we last spoke."

"Has it?" Yamani retorted. "I hadn't noticed."

"Yamani!" Queen Xandria said crossly. "We came all this way to discuss a matter of huge importance to you. The least you could do is listen."

"Oh, now you care about what is of importance to me?" Yamani rolled her eyes and shook her head.

Zäria had never seen her queen act this way. She was surprised that Yamani would speak to another queen in this manner.

Suddenly, Queen Yamani stepped back, appearing confused. "Why is Ambrosia with you? What's this all about, Mother?"

Zäria gasped loudly. *The king and queen of Ellyngshyme are Queen Yamani's parents!* She suddenly felt all eyes on her. "Sorry," she said, looking down at her feet.

Yamani swiftly stepped past her royal parents and hugged Zäria. This too was behavior the queen usually did not exhibit. "Zäria and Avery, I have been losing sleep with worry, awaiting your return." Her look of concern turned to anger as she faced Queen Xandria, "Why was I not alerted immediately of their safety?"

"That is exactly why we have come in person, dear," Queen Xandria said. "There are also some other matters that need to come to light."

King Byron approached his daughter. "Yamani," he said softly, placing his hand on her shoulder, "from what the young fae have told us, I fear that Thordon is really up to something. Your mother and I feel it is time to put an end to this feud."

Yamani pushed King Byron's hand away from her shoulder. "You want to put an end to the feud you created?" Zäria could see the hurt in Yamani's eyes with a flash of anger. Queen Yamani took a deep breath and then displayed the cool and calm demeanor that Zäria was accustomed to seeing. "Zäria, please tell me that you retrieved the seed you were sent after."

"Yes." Zäria nodded at Ambrosia, who placed a hand on her gold satchel. "Ambrosia has it safe in her satchel, protected by magic."

"Then we mustn't waste our time here," Yamani declared. "We need to deliver the seed to Thordon so he will allow my faeries to return to Saizia unharmed."

"Yes, we have sat idle for too long." King Byron reached out his arm to Yamani. "Come, dear, you will ride with your mother and me."

Yamani glowered at the king but headed to the carriage, as instructed. Zäria quietly followed alongside the carriage with Avery and the guards.

After the tense reunion, Zäria's nerves were even more unsettled about the impending meeting with Thordon. She still did not know what he was up to or just how dangerous he could be. She hoped he would keep his word and let her and Avery return home unharmed. She began to get chills as they passed the first few trees into Eerie Hollow. Her wings were noticeably shivering.

Avery held her hand to calm her and whispered, "Everything will work out, Zär."

She could only nod in reply. *I will never set foot in Eerie Hollow again,* she promised herself, *if I make it out of this mess with my wings intact.*

The familiar aroma of chocolate triggered another of Zäria's strange new visions—she saw Thordon flying like a faerie, which was weird since she didn't remember his having wings. The sound of rustling in the nearby bushes pulled her out of her vision and back into the hollow.

Two elves popped out in front of her from either side. "Gus, alert the guards!" one yelled over his shoulder. The other added, "Trespassers!" The portly elf wobbled as fast as his stubby little legs could carry him away from her group until he disappeared into a cavern up ahead. The royal guards encircled the royal family and stood ready to react.

Gus returned with two armed guards in tow. His speech was a bit broken as he was out of breath. "Thordon wishes to … meet with you … inside. Please follow me." He waved to the group and then turned to the other elves. "Bean, Sprout, get back to work!"

Zäria managed to stifle her laughter as the two elves stumbled over each other. She joined the royal family as they alighted from the carriage and followed Thordon's minions into the cave. Zäria got the heebie-jeebies being back within the cave walls. It reminded her of being in the Lost Room. Even the smell of chocolate would forever be ruined for her. If Avery was just as scared, he didn't let it show. *Boys are better at hiding that sort of thing*, she thought.

Zäria noticed there wasn't as much activity as during their last visit. In fact, it was eerily quiet inside the halls, except for the echoes of their own shuffling feet along the damp cave floors. The guard led them through a wide doorway into a spacious room with impossibly high ceilings. Zäria thought perhaps it was more faerie magic or that they were traveling downhill. A massive round table in the center of the room was surrounded by wooden stools. One stool was larger than the rest and shaped more like a throne. *That's obviously for Thordon*, she thought, *to accommodate his large ego.*

She took a seat next to Avery on a small wooden bench along the wall in the back of the room and watched as King Byron and Queens Xandria and Yamani sat at the table. The small wooden stools were obviously not built for royalty, but the king and queen did their best to keep their composure.

Light crept in as a door opened on the other side of the room. In walked two of Thordon's elven guards. Zäria felt chills down her spine as Thordon made his entrance and took his place at the table in the throne-like chair. The creepy dwarfs sat on either side of him.

King Byron and Queen Xandria sat directly across from Thordon. The rest of the group filled in the remaining seats. Their guards stood behind them.

Thordon silently looked over the group one by one, sizing them up. Finally, he spoke. "I was not expecting such grand company at this meeting. I hope these accommodations suit your needs."

"The venue is of no importance as long as we are able to discuss the matter at hand," replied Queen Xandria.

"Yes, indeed," added King Byron.

"I'm glad we all agree. Now where is my seed?" asked Thordon.

Zäria instinctively looked at Ambrosia, which Thordon noticed.

He yelled at Ambrosia, "Do you have my seed, old woman?"

Ambrosia did not answer.

"I assure you that the young fae completed the task you required of them," King Byron interjected. "The seed is safe and will be given to you once we have come to an agreement."

"Nonsense!" Thordon shouted. "The agreement was a seed for the fae's freedom. No seed, no wings. Guards, apprehend those faeries and cut off their wings!"

Zäria clung to Avery's arms as Thordon's guards grabbed hold of her. Drovak quickly drew his sword and rested it on the throat of one of the guards.

King Byron stood up and shouted, "Stop this at once, Thordon! Call off your guards. We brought your damned seed, and we demand a civil meeting!"

Zäria jumped as King Byron slammed his heavy hand on the wooden table with a loud thump. Thordon waived his guards off, and Zäria curled herself into Avery's arm as the guards released them. She heard shuffling as everyone returned to their seats. Next she heard King Byron's voice.

"I know we have not seen eye to eye in the past. Queen Xandria and I need to set some things straight before discussing anything further." He took a brief pause. "The faerie pact was enacted with our villages' futures in mind, but it may not have been the best resolution. Now it seems like an ancient notion to uphold."

"Yes, that nasty pact has caused some dismal affairs over the years, hasn't it?" Thordon said snidely. He briefly glanced at Yamani, and she looked away.

Queen Xandria added, "We feel it is time to release the pact and form an alliance, if you will."

Thordon snorted. "Break the pact, you say?"

"Yes, exactly. Fae and elves and all creatures may coexist in harmony." Queen Xandria sighed heavily. "The king and I were not very fair to you in our quest to do what we thought was best for the future of our kingdom. We see that now. Lives have been put at stake, and continuing the pact now will do more harm than good."

"*Now* it will do more harm than good?" Yamani asked. "I don't remember that pact doing anyone any good since the seal was put on it."

"What is the point of this?" Thordon thundered. "Just hand over the seed, and we can be done with this!"

Queen Xandria quickly stood and shouted, "The point is that Zäria is not just any faerie who stumbled upon you. She is your daughter, Thordon!"

"Mother!" Yamani cried. "How could you blurt that out with Zäria in the room?"

Queen Xandria threw her hand to her mouth. "Zäria, I'm so sorry, dear. My anger got the better of me, I'm afraid."

Zäria was paralyzed with shock as she stared at Thordon in horror. She felt the points of her ears burn and knew they were turning red. Her heart was beating so hard that she was sure everyone could hear it in the now-silent room. Zäria had grown accustomed to not knowing who her real parents were, but for Thordon to be her father was just too much to bear. She would rather have not known at all.

Thordon looked at Yamani with anger and hurt. "All these years I thought our daughter was dead. Did you know?"

Yamani was completely sobbing now. "I had no choice once the pact was made. Zäria was sent to live outside the palace and was to never know we were her parents, Thordon."

King Byron added, "Once Zäria's life was put in danger, we felt you needed to know the truth, and it was time to break the pact."

"Breaking this pact now is not going to undo the damage it has already done. It's like putting a bandage on a severed hand and hoping it will grow back." Thordon shook his head. "I don't think even your faerie magic could do that."

"Perhaps you're right, Thordon, but what's done is done. We cannot take it back, but we can end it now," King Byron replied. "That is what we came here to do."

"The only thing that concerns me is that seed. Give me the seed, and I don't care what you do with the pact," Thordon said angrily.

"That brings me to the next matter at hand," King Byron said.

"What else could there possibly be? You are wearing my patience thin with your matters of so-called importance," Thordon said scornfully.

"Eguin," the king said.

"What do you want with my dragon?" Thordon demanded.

Rorik stepped forward angrily, but Drovak put his arm out to stop him. Thordon smirked at the guard. Zäria was reminded of Rorik's anger toward Avery for making the same faux pas of calling Eguin "Thordon's dragon."

"I'm sure you are aware that Eguin is the dwarfs' dragon," King Byron corrected. "Rorik here"—he pointed to the guard—"was his primary caregiver. Eguin should be returned to his rightful home in Ellyngshyme."

Thordon crossed his arms over his chest. "No."

"I'm not asking permission, Thordon. Return the dragon so Rorik and the other dwarfs can properly care for him."

"All right, Byron. I will return the dragon to Ellyngshyme. First, you give me the seed." Thordon put his hand out.

"What is the purpose of this seed you are so eager to acquire?" King Byron asked.

"It is of a personal nature," Thordon responded. "I do not wish to discuss it with you. I went through a lot of trouble to obtain it, and I do not intend to allow you to leave with it."

"And I have no intention of leaving you with a possible weapon, Thordon."

"Weapon? It's a seed, for fox's sake," retorted Thordon. "I intend to plant it."

King Byron took a moment to think about his response and then said, "Very well. Ambrosia, give Thordon the seed."

The sorceress removed the golden satchel from around her neck and removed the seed. She looked at King Byron before placing the tiny seed in Thordon's hand.

Thordon snatched it up and began to examine it. "Funny. I didn't expect it to look so ordinary. Now I must ask you all to leave Eerie Hollow at once."

"Not without the dragon, half-elf," Rorik spat.

"You'll get your dragon when I'm done with him, dwarf. Let's say in a fortnight."

Queen Xandria placed her hand on Rorik's armor-clad arm to restrain him. "That sounds like a reasonable amount of time to comply, Thordon," she said. Rorik returned to his seat.

King Byron nodded. "Yes, that will do. And I believe it is time we adjourned to our homes."

Zäria stood up, ready to leave with the others, when she noticed that Queen Yamani remained seated.

Queen Xandria asked, "Is everything all right, Yamani?"

"I think I'm going to stay behind. Thordon and I have some things to discuss further."

"Do you wish us to stay?" asked the king.

"No, this is of a private nature. Thank you for your concern, but I will be fine."

"Very well," said Queen Xandria, "but please keep Drovak as an escort home."

"Yes, Mother. I will. Safe travels home."

Once the royal party had withdrawn from the room, Yamani asked Drovak to wait outside the door for her. She kept him to appease her mother but wanted to keep her conversation with Thordon private.

Yamani and Thordon sat in awkward silence for a few minutes, looking at each other across the table. Yamani sat with her elbows on the table, hands clasped, and her chin resting upon them. She took a deep breath and set her hands on the table in front of her. "What was all that about with the seed, Thordon?"

"That is really none of your concern."

"I hope it has nothing to do with revenge against my faeries." She watched his eyes for telltale signs of deceit.

"I have no intention of harming you, Yamani. I am insulted. Do you not remember me at all? Do you remember us?"

"That was a long time ago, Thordon, but I remember. I also remember your imprisoning two young fae and sending them on a dangerous quest for your benefit, one of them our daughter. So I'm not sure who you are now."

Thordon stood and walked around the table to Yamani. He pulled out the chair next to her and sat facing her. He grabbed both her hands in his. Yamani almost pulled away but stopped herself and grasped his hands as well. "That pact ..." He shook his head. "It made me so angry. It took you away from me, and when rumor came to me that our child was dead ... I became hardened to dull the pain. You're right. I did change. Then today, all the things taken from me were laid at my feet. It will take time to mend what was broken, but I will try."

Yamani let go of Thordon's hands and pushed her chair back as she stood from the table. "It was a shock to me as well, after years of pushing all my feelings aside. Duties of being a queen were a great distraction."

"You used to appreciate distraction," he said. He made a red rose appear in his hand and offered it to her.

She was reminded of when Thordon had entertained her with the faerie magic he was able to master. She hated that it still made her smile. She took the rose and set it on the table. "I'm not a young girl anymore. I can't be won with simple faerie magic. I have a kingdom that depends on me now. There are many things to be considered."

Thordon grimaced. "I'm still not good enough? Not faerish enough for you, Yamani?"

"I have never thought less of you for being half elf, Thordon. Don't try to bring me down that path. I'm saying the good of my people needs to be first and foremost. I think it is time for me to go."

"Yes, return to Saizia. There is much for you to ponder. I too need some time." He escorted her to the door and let her out.

Yamani met Drovak, who was waiting for her in the hallway.

"Ready, Your Majesty?"

"Yes, I wish to return to Saizia." She nodded a goodbye to Thordon and went on her way with her guard. Her heart was heavy. *This is like reliving the pain of losing Thordon and Zäria all over again,* she thought. She replayed the scenarios of the past and the present through her head all the way back to her palace.

CHAPTER 12

Royalty

äria was relieved to see Yamani enter the palace. She was worried about her safety when she was left alone with Thordon.

King Byron rejoiced. "Ah, Yamani. You have safely returned. Your mother and I thought it best to escort the young fae to the palace and to be sure of your safety before we returned to Ellyngshyme. Is everything in order with Thordon?"

"Yes, everything is in order," she replied. "May I have a private word with you and Mother?"

"Of course you may." He waved a hand to Queen Xandria. "Come, dear; let's have a chat with Yamani."

Yamani turned to Zäria and Avery. "Excuse us for a moment. We have some details to clarify. Please stay. I want to speak with you both as well."

"Yes, Your Majesty," replied Avery as he bowed.

"No need for all the formality, Avery. We'll be but a moment. Thank you." As she walked toward the study, she said, "Poppy, please bring us some dandelion tea and honey."

"Yes, Your Highness, straightaway." The attendant quickly flew to the kitchen.

Zäria was disappointed she would yet again have to wait to have her questions answered. She felt like everyone made her life decisions without consulting her. She watched as the mother she longed to know disappeared into the study and closed the doors behind her. A few moments later, Poppy returned with the tea and honey on a tray. She nodded at Zäria and Avery and rang the bell to request entry to the room. The door creaked open, and Poppy entered the room and closed the door behind her.

Now that the young fae were alone in the quiet room, they realized just how drained they were from this adventure. They sat on the settee near a large stack of books. Zäria picked up the book on top, titled *Human History and Other Mistakes to Learn From*. She opened it to the midsection and silently read a passage at random.

"Wow, glad I haven't encountered any of these human creatures. They do a lot of dumb stuff," she said as she closed the book and set it back on the table.

Avery sighed and closed his eyes. Zäria nudged his arm when he began to snore. He woke with a start. "Zär, what's wrong? Is Weezelbet back?" He looked around, and Zäria laughed as he turned a bit red when he noticed where he was.

"You were snoring like a bull frog."

"Oh, sorry. I'm just so tired." He stood up, stretched his wings, and then flew around in a couple of small circles. He straightened out and flew straight up to the ceiling, did a back flip, and swooped back down.

Zäria ducked to avoid Avery's crashing into her. "You're going to get us both in trouble, Avery." No sooner had she finished her sentence than the royal family entered the room, and Yamani had no choice but to quickly duck when she saw Avery flying in her direction.

"Avery Lightfoot!" Queen Yamani shouted. "What are you doing, flying in my palace? You almost knocked me over."

He stumbled in making his landing and fell into a heap on the floor. Zäria was embarrassed for him as she helped him up.

"Please forgive me" Avery said. "I do apologize, Your Majesty. I was only stretching my wings, but I got carried away." Avery's cheeks turned all shades of red.

"Indoors, Avery? You know better than that." She smoothed out her gown and straightened her hair and then took a deep breath. "Oh, there was no harm done. Just don't let it happen again. Avery, you are free to go home and rest. We need to talk to Zäria alone."

"Getting back to my own bed is exactly what I want to do right now. Thank you, Your Highness." He bowed to the queen and turned to Zäria. "You can stop by any time, Zär. I'll see you later."

She waved at him as he headed out of the palace. Queen Yamani gestured for Zäria to sit down on the settee. The two queens took a seat on the sofa across from her, and the king sat in a chair to their right.

Zäria felt very nervous with all of them staring at her and without Avery by her side. She was thankful when Yamani broke the awkward silence.

"Zäria, now that your true identity has been revealed, it is only fair to offer you your rightful place in the royal family. You are a princess and heir to the throne. Queen Xandria, King Byron, and I have discussed this, and we feel it should be up to you whether you move into the palace here in Saizia or move to the sanctuary of Ellyngshyme."

It had never occurred to Zäria that she would need to move out of the only home she had known, much less decide which kingdom she wanted to live in. "Do I have to choose? Can't I just stay in my own house?"

"You are a princess, Zäria," King Byron reminded her.

She nodded but said, "I really want to go home to my own bed."

"Of course, dear," agreed Queen Yamani. "This has been a lot all at once, for everyone." She turned to her parents. "We should let Zäria rest, and we can discuss this later."

King Byron let out a soft sigh. "Very well; agreed. Zäria, you are welcome at Ellyngshyme any time."

Everyone stood. Queen Xandria moved closer to Zäria and brushed a strand of hair back behind her right ear. "It has been good to know you, dear."

Zäria wished she could have known the queen as her grandmother. She seemed to be very caring.

"Zäria I am allowing you to return to the comfort of your own bed," Yamani advised, "but I'm sending one of my guards with you. It soon will be known that you are royalty, and Thordon's intentions are uncertain. Your life could be in danger." The queen sighed. "I'm worried for you, dear." She took a seat next to Zäria on the couch. "There was a time when I trusted Thordon with my life. Maybe my parents were right to keep us apart after all. I hope you understand that I never wanted this for you. I resented my parents for taking you away from me to be raised outside the palace. I always watched over you and checked in on you. I now have the opportunity to really get to know you, to be a proper mother to you. I know I cannot give back the years spent apart, but I do hope you will consider moving into the palace."

Zäria felt overwhelmed. "Thank you for all your kindness, Your Majesty. I am very exhausted and a bit out of sorts. I would really like to rest and think about it—that is, if it's all right with you."

"Of course it's all right with me. I will send two of my guards to escort you home and stand post outside until morning. Please return tomorrow night so we may continue this discussion."

"You have my word." With that, Zäria departed with the two guards. As they approached the palace gate, Zäria could see curious faeries gathered together. They whispered and gawked at her. She felt awkward and embarrassed to have the guards escort her past the inquisitive stares.

Zäria was relieved to see her quaint little home. She went inside and left the guards outside her door. She was finally alone with her thoughts. She looked around. Everything was as she'd left it days ago—her breakfast dishes on the table, the picnic basket she had used for her and Avery's lunch, her bed unmade. She curled up on her bed, pulled her bedclothes up to her cold little nose, and fell fast asleep.

Morning came, and Zäria woke with a start. She had dreamed she was in the Lost Room and went into a panic. She must have let out an involuntary scream because one of the royal guards burst in, asking "Are you all right, Your Royal Highness?"

"Royal what?" she asked while wiping the sleep out of her eyes.

She looked around and realized she was in her own room, and she was no longer dreaming. She let out another scream, startled to see a royal guard standing in front of her. He stuck out like a sore thumb in her pastel room.

"Your Royal Highness. You are the Princess Zäria, are you not?" asked the guard.

Zäria definitely was not prepared to be referred to as royalty, with guards following her around.

"Well, yes, I guess I am. I'm just not used to it. Nor am I used to guards bursting into my bedroom. Could you please give me a bit of privacy?"

The guard's cheeks turned red. "Forgive me, Princess Zäria. I forgot my manners. It won't happen again." He bowed and stumbled over his own foot as he exited the room.

Zäria slipped out of bed, stretched a few times, and fluttered the sleep from her wings. It really was nice to wake up at home, guards and all. She was finally able to bathe and change her clothes. After attending to her morning ablutions, she spent some time attempting to coordinate an outfit to wear. She was having trouble finding something royal but not obviously snobby. She wondered if orange blossoms or blue forget-me-nots said that better. After trying on everything in her house, including her curtains as a royal robe and a serving bowl as a crown, she finally settled on her pink rose-petal dress with baby's breath in her plaited hair. Just as she was fitting her foot into her favorite shoes, the guard tapped on her door.

Zäria opened the door. "Thank you for knocking, which is so much better."

"Yes, Your Majesty. You have a guest calling to see you." He stepped aside to reveal a confused Avery behind him.

"Oh, Avery, never mind them. Come in." Zäria turned around and gestured for him to follow her into the kitchen.

Avery nodded at each guard and hopped past them into the house, where he took a seat at her kitchen table. "What's with the heavy security, Zär?" he asked while digging through the picnic basket, looking for snacks.

Zäria took the empty basket and moved it out of the way as she took a seat across the table for Avery. "Oh, Queen Yamani ..." She paused to correct herself. "My mother insisted."

Avery raised an eyebrow. "Your mother, the queen. That is going to take some getting used to. Should I start bowing in your presence, Your Highness?" He stood and took a dramatic bow.

"Don't be snide, Avery. Why are you here?"

"Where else should I be?"

"I don't know. Tending the toadstools, maybe?"

Avery scoffed at that. "The toadstools can wait. Food comes first. Do you have anything to eat? I'm starving."

Zäria rolled her eyes and shook her head. "Is that seriously all you think about, Avery Lightfoot?" When he shrugged, Zäria stood up and began hunting through her cupboards and drawers for anything edible. "Looks like we need to go find some grub. We've been gone a while."

"Can't you just ask your new friends to get us something?"

She thought about it for a moment. *I might as well make the most of being a royal princess.* "I can do better than that," she said, "Let's go eat at the palace."

"Eat at the palace? I don't know ... we had that last week."

Zäria shot Avery a dirty look.

"Kidding! Let's go to the palace."

They walked out the door to find the two guards still standing in silence. "We would like to go to the palace," Zäria said with what she thought was an authoritative tone.

The guards simply nodded, and the four of them took flight. Zäria was not used to things being so easy for her. *Perhaps living in the palace would not be such a bad idea.*

"News sure travels fast in Saizia," Avery said as he looked down at the faeries they passed along the way. "Look—they are all bowing to you, Zäria."

Her cheeks flushed. "This is a bit overwhelming and awkward, having everyone gawking at me."

Being royal did have its perks, though. The guards walked

through the gates and escorted the faeries straight into the palace. Guards and staff all bowed to Zäria as she passed.

Poppy was the first to greet them at the door. She bowed and said, "Good morrow, Your Highness. Her Majesty, the queen, will be pleased you have returned so promptly. Shall I announce your arrival?"

"That won't be necessary, Poppy. I don't want to disturb Yamani. Would it be too much trouble for us to breakfast here this morning?" Zäria asked.

Poppy clapped her hands together in excitement. "No trouble at all. You are just in time to join the queen. We just finished dressing the table. Please follow me to the dining room." She spun around and waved for them to follow. They adjourned down a hallway gracefully decorated with jewels, just as was the rest of the palace they had seen so far. They soon entered a room with chairs covered in pink silk arranged around a large table, which was covered with a scrumptious-smelling feast. "Sit anywhere you like, and I will let the queen know you will be joining her." With that, Poppy left them on their own.

The two fae picked chairs in the center of the table and sat down. Avery reached for a blueberry, but Zäria quickly slapped his hand.

"We can't eat before the queen arrives. That is rude, Avery."

He rubbed his hand. "Sorry. I'm hungry, and it's just one berry."

Zäria didn't bother to respond; she heard the chatter of approaching voices. The door opened, and in walked Poppy with three faeries behind her. She stayed behind as the faeries took their seats at the table across from Avery and Zäria. There was an awkward silence for a moment as they all looked at each other. Poppy peeked her head out the door and announced, "She's here." The three faeries rose, so Avery and Zäria followed suit. Poppy held open the door as Queen Yamani stepped through, dressed in a pink-peony gown, with lavender tangled into her hair and silver crown. All bowed as she made her way to her seat at the head of the table.

Once everyone was seated, the queen smiled at Zäria. "It pleases me to see you at the palace for breakfast. Allow me to introduce you to everyone." She pointed to the faerie closest to her. Her lined face told that she was older than the queen; her golden hair was streaked with silver and gray. "This is my royal adviser, Orla." Orla nodded at Avery and Zäria. "Beside her is Veena. She is Saizia's royal sorceress and the granddaughter of Ambrosia, my mother's sorceress in Ellyngshyme."

"Is Goran your father?" Zäria blurted out.

Veena shook her head. "No, he is my uncle. My mother passed."

Zäria's cheeks became flushed. "Oh, I am so sorry. I didn't mean ..."

"No harm," Veena said.

Yamani continued her introductions. "There, at the end of the table, is Holvar. He is the commander of the Royal Guard."

He certainly fits that role, Zäria thought. He was the largest faerie Zäria had ever seen. He had dark-red hair and a long beard to match. His face was fierce and his eyes a piercing blue. He merely grunted in acknowledgment of the introduction, which made the young fae flinch.

"Manners, Holvar," the queen reprimanded. She then addressed those gathered around the table. "Everyone, let me formally introduce to you my daughter, Princess Zäria."

In unison, the three faeries said, "Your Majesty," and bowed their heads to her.

Yamani waved her hand in Avery's direction. "And her companion, Avery Lightfoot, son of Theadora and Aerion Lightfoot." She took her napkin from the table and placed it in her lap. "Okay, enough introductions. Let's eat, shall we?"

Everyone picked up their tableware and began to eat. Avery had seconds and then thirds.

"Hungry, Avery?" Zäria asked with a giggle.

Avery wiped his mouth with the back of his hand and then rested it on his full stomach. He let out a sigh. "That was the best food I ever tasted. I think I ate more than I meant to. Thank you, Your Majesties."

Yamani smiled at Avery. "I am glad that you enjoyed your breakfast, Avery. You are more than welcome at the palace any time."

Poppy and a few other attendants cleared the table and refilled tea cups with fresh dandelion tea.

"I had intended to discuss recent events with my advisers, but I do think the two of you should stay. It does pertain to you as well," the queen said to Avery and Zäria.

Zäria hadn't realized their breakfast would include being involved in important matters of the kingdom, but she supposed it came with the territory. "Yes, Your Highness."

"No need to be so formal, dear," Yamani replied. "Veena, I believe it is time to remove the vow-of-silence charm on Millie."

Veena jerked her head up from her tea cup, nearly spilling it on herself. "Your Majesty, are you sure that is wise?"

"Yes. That charm was the only way we could protect her and the pact. Since the pact has been abolished, and Eerie Hollow is no longer a secret to Saizia, I feel it is time to give her voice back." She turned to Avery. "Veena will need toadstools to make the antidote to remove the charm. See to it that she has all that she needs."

"Yes, of course, Your Majesty."

"Veena, once you have restored Millie's voice, bring her to me. We have a lot to discuss."

Veena bowed her head. "As you wish. I will start at once." She lifted her head to address Avery. "Please bring three toadstools to the palace. Tell Persephani what it is for. She will know what I need."

"I will," replied Avery. "Should I go now, Your Majesty?"

"Not just yet. You may go once we adjourn our meeting. Holvar, have your guards prepare for the worst. I am still uncertain of Thordon's intentions at this point. I want to be ready for anything."

"Of course, Your Majesty." Holvar bowed his head to her.

"I agree with Queen Yamani," said Orla. "We need to be vigilant."

Feeling out of place, Zäria just nodded in agreement.

Yamani stood up. "Then it is settled. This meeting is adjourned until this evening. Avery, please make haste to see Persephani. Veena, start working on that potion immediately. I will have Poppy bring Millie to you. Zäria, you will stay with me."

Poppy quickly assisted the queen with her robes and moved the chair out of her way. The queen motioned to Zäria to follow, and they exited the dining hall, leaving the rest of the party to go their separate ways.

CHAPTER 13

Secrets

Zäria was nervous about why Yamani had asked her to stay. She still felt out of place at the palace. She followed the queen down a winding hallway, away from the others in the dining hall. The walls were not as shimmery as in the rest of the palace, and the light seemed to dim the farther they went. At last they came to a large doorway that led into a room filled with books and scrolls. Yamani quietly walked to the far side of the room near the small fireplace. She waved her hand in front of it, and a warm fire crackled. The chill of the room quickly dissipated. The queen pointed to a small table and chairs near the fire.

"Please sit, Zäria. We have a lot of catching up to do."

As Zäria took a seat at the table, she heard a noise behind her. Poppy had come in with warm dandelion tea and honey. She set them on the table and served the tea.

"Thank you, Poppy," the queen said. "Let Holvar know where we are and that no one is to disturb us unless absolutely necessary. That will be all."

Poppy silently bowed her head to the queen and then again to Zäria before leaving the room.

Yamani took a small sip of her tea and set the cup back on the table. "This is Saizia's library, where all important documents are kept. Only the royal family is allowed access to these books and scrolls.

Here, you can find information about everyone in our family, back to the time Saizia came to be."

"There are so many books. I'm not sure where I would start," Zäria said, feeling a bit overwhelmed.

"Yes, in time you may look deeper into our history. For now, I suggest starting with this book." She waved her hand in the air, and a book bound in pinkish moleskin appeared in her hand. Yamani set the book on the table, opened it to the last page with writing on it, and pushed it toward Zäria.

Zäria looked at the open page. Its delicate writing read, *Born to Princess Yamani and Thordon, Duke of Eerie Hollow—Zäria, Princess of Saizia.*

Zäria stared at the page for a moment and then looked up at the queen in surprise. "Is there a book about me as well?"

"Not yet," replied the queen. "I added that part after the pact was broken. I have ordered the recordkeepers to begin your book." She closed the book in front of them. "You are welcome to read any book you choose, as long as nothing leaves this vault. I must excuse myself to attend to a few items while you learn some of our history. I will return shortly. Call upon Poppy if you need anything in my absence."

"Yes, Your Majesty. Thank you."

After Yamani left the room, Zäria opened the book to the first page and began reading about her royal family. She noticed that all the females in the family line were named in alphabetical order: her great-grandmother, Willow, followed by her grandmother, Xandria; her mother, Yamani; and then her own name, Zäria.

Interesting.

Poppy entered the vault. "Is there anything I can do for you, Princess Zäria?"

"No, thank you, Poppy."

"Very well. Please just ring the bell if you change your mind."

"I will."

With that, Poppy left the room.

Zäria continued reading through the book. She was in the vault alone for a long while. She kept herself entertained by peeking into several of the other books on the shelves. She couldn't believe how much she hadn't known about Saizia.

Zäria was beginning to wonder if Yamani was coming back. She had grown tired and hungry after reading for so long. She rang the bell on the table.

Poppy appeared moments later. "Yes, Your Majesty?"

"I'm beginning to feel hungry. Do you know when Yamani will return?"

"The queen's lunch is about to be served in the dining hall, if you wish to eat."

"Yes, that will be perfect."

Poppy escorted Zäria to the dining hall. Faeries were still setting the table, but the queen had not yet arrived. Zäria sat at the table, and Poppy poured some water for her.

Without warning, Yamani stormed into the room in a huff. Her eyes were narrowed and her lips pursed. She fluttered her wings and then straightened them out so they were stiff as she marched to her seat at the table. "Zäria, I apologize for leaving you for such a long time in the vault." The anger in Yamani's voice was clear.

"It's all right. I learned a lot while you were gone. Is everything okay?"

Queen Yamani let out a sigh to calm herself. "Yes. I'm quite well. I am only ill-tempered because I went to check on Veena's progress on the antidote, and she wasn't in her potions room. It appears she has yet to begin." She took a drink from the acorn goblet in front of her. She made a face and quickly set it back down. "Water? Poppy, fetch me some of your blackberry mead."

"Of course, Your Majesty." Poppy bowed and scurried off to the kitchen. She returned with a small clay decanter with blackberry vines painted on it. She filled a goblet for the queen and another for Zäria.

Zäria had never tasted mead. She waited for Yamani to take a drink before she picked up her own goblet. The dark-red brew smelled pungent and sweet. She took a sip. The bubbles tickled her nose, and the drink made her tongue tingle. She took a bigger drink.

"Careful, Zäria. Poppy's mead will sneak up on you with a big kick to the head if you imbibe too much too quickly." The queen took a small sip in demonstration and then set her goblet on the table. "Now, tell me—did you learn anything while reading in the vault?"

"Oh yes, but still so much more to read."

"Very good. You are welcome to enter the vault as often as you like." Yamani took a bite of the food set before her and another sip of mead before calling to Poppy. "Poppy, please bring Millie to the dining hall. We will feed her before checking to see if Veena has returned to her potions room."

Poppy bowed to the queen, "Yes, Your Majesty." After a brief time, Poppy returned with Millie, who silently made her way to the table, bowed to the queen, and took a seat. Poppy filled a goblet with water and another with mead, and she also set a plate of food in front of Millie.

"Millie," Queen Yamani said, "I have asked you here because I feel it is time to remove the vow of silence that was placed on you."

Millie choked on her drink in surprise and quickly wiped her face with her napkin. It was obvious she had many questions. A big smile crept across her face, and she stood up, ready to go.

"Oh no, Millie, not quite yet. Have a seat."

The smile on Millie's face was replaced with disappointment. She returned to her chair and pushed the food around on her plate.

"Don't look so forlorn, dear. Veena hasn't finished the antidote yet. You should eat a bit, and then we will escort you to her."

After they all had finished their meals, the queen stood up from the table and advised Millie and Zäria to accompany her to the potions room. Veena still was not there. "We will wait for her here," said the queen.

Millie and Zäria sat down in the window seat and watched Yamani pace back and forth.

A few moments later, the door creaked open, and a startled Veena walked in. She put her hand on her chest and tried to slow her breathing. "Your Majesty, you gave me quite a fright. I was not expecting anyone to be awaiting me."

"I instructed you to begin working on this antidote immediately. Where were you, Veena?"

"I needed fennel root, and Avery had not yet returned with the toadstools, so I went to fetch them myself." She raised her left hand to show the raw roots in the basket she was carrying. She set the basket on a small table in the center of the room.

"Avery should be returning any moment, and you now have your fennel root. Let us not delay this any further."

"Of course, Your Majesty. I will begin brewing the antidote right away." Veena hung a black cauldron of water over the fireplace and waved her hand to conjure a crackling fire. She threw in the fennel and dumped the contents of a few of her potions bottles into the cauldron and stirred. She let go of the spoon and dusted her hands on her skirt.

Zäria heard footsteps, and the door creaked. She looked up to see Avery enter the room.

"Here are the toadstools you asked for, Veena," Avery said as he rolled the toadstools over to her.

"Perfect. Just throw them directly into the fire, Avery."

The toadstools made the fire grow, and it started to glow bright blue and then flashed white for a few seconds.

"I need to pull a hair from your head," Veena said to Millie. She then tossed the hair into the cauldron. After stirring the brew a few times, she announced it was finished. She spooned a bit into a cup and handed it to Millie. "Drink."

Millie sniffed the concoction and winced. She closed her eyes and took a drink. Veena quickly put her hand on the bottom of the cup and tilted it back to make sure Millie continued to drink. When she finally let go, Millie dropped the cup and wiped her mouth several times on the scarf that was hanging around her neck.

"Yuck!" she yelled and then reflexively put her hands to her mouth. "I can talk!" She jumped up. "I have missed my voice." She threw her arms around Veena's neck and squeezed her tightly. "Thank you."

Veena pulled away. "Don't thank me. I only did what the queen requested."

Millie dropped to her knees and bowed all the way to the ground at the queen's feet. "Thank you, Your Majesty."

"Come now, Millie. We have lots to discuss." Yamani motioned to her to stand up. Yamani walked out of the potions room with Millie in tow. Zäria stared at the basket on the table.

Avery nudged her arm. "Let's go, Zäria."

She shook herself out of the trance and followed Avery from the room. When they'd put a bit of distance between them and the potions room, Zäria whispered to Avery, "Did you see what was in Veena's basket?"

"Yeah, fennel."

"*Under* the fennel." She rolled her eyes. "It was chocolate, Avery."

"So?"

"So where do you think she got it?"

"You don't think … she got it from Thordon, do you?"

"Yes. I remember the first time we went to Eerie Hollow. We heard the two elves teasing Gus about liking someone named Veena."

"What are you two whispering about?" Yamani asked crossly.

Avery and Zäria stopped in their tracks and looked at each other without saying a thing.

"I asked a question, and I expect an answer," the queen said sternly with her arms crossed.

"Did you notice that Veena had chocolate underneath the fennel in her basket, Your Majesty?" asked Zäria.

The queen raised an eyebrow. "What is the relevance of it?"

"Avery and I were discussing where Veena might have collected such chocolate. We think she went to Eerie Hollow."

Rage flashed in the queen's eyes. Without saying a word, she stormed past the young fae and toward the potions room.

Zäria grabbed Avery's arm and dragged him along behind Queen Yamani. "I want to see what she's going to do," Zäria said.

The queen barged through the door and snatched the basket off the table, dumping out its contents. The chocolates rolled across the table and onto the floor. Yamani looked at Veena, who was speechless and frozen in shock.

"Chocolates!" the queen shouted. "What were you doing in Eerie Hollow, Veena?"

"Collecting fennel, like I told you earlier, Your Majesty," Veena retorted.

"You failed to mention you were in Eerie Hollow. Did you get these chocolates from Thordon?"

"Of course not."

"Do not lie to me, Veena."

"I got the chocolates from one of the elves who made them. He gave them to me when I was picking the fennel."

Yamani took a deep breath to calm herself. "With all that is going on, you should not be venturing into Eerie Hollow alone."

"Yes, Your Majesty. I will take a chaperone if ever I need anything from there in the future." Veena bent down to pick up the chocolates and fennel, returning them to the basket.

Queen Yamani turned on her heel and ushered Zäria and Avery ahead of her through the door. She called back to Veena, "If I find out that you are conspiring with Thordon in any way, Veena, it will be your head you are chasing on the floor."

Zäria was shocked to hear Yamani utter such a vicious threat. She silently followed the queen down the hall so as to not upset her further.

"Zäria and Avery, you are also free to go, if you please," Yamani said.

"Thank you." Zäria felt they had been in the palace long enough for the day. With all the information they had learned, they could not wait to get somewhere and talk freely. They both let out a sigh of relief after they were standing outside the palace gates.

CHAPTER 14

The Spell

n Eerie Hollow, Sprout was busy daydreaming.

"Sprout, don't just stand there. Move some carts to storage or something," Gus barked.

"Oh, sorry, I was just thinking," replied Sprout.

"Well, don't hurt yourself," Bean joked as he let out a laugh.

Gus nudged him in the side with his elbow. "Good one, Bean."

Sprout grabbed the handles of an empty cart and pushed past the two jokesters. He was tired of always being the butt of their jokes. "Ha-ha. You're both a barrel of laughs today."

Still laughing, Gus replied, "Maybe you should check if Thordon needs anything and let him know we are almost done packing up the chocolates."

"Anything to get away from you two," Sprout said and headed into the cavern after absentmindedly grabbing the empty cart. After a moment, he realized he was still pushing the cart. He handed it over to a passing elf and continued to Eguin's cavern.

He reached the door to the cavern, which was slightly ajar. He found Thordon planting the seed he'd gotten from the faeries in a large clay pot. Thordon chanted a spell and poured a potion on it. The seed sprouted into a leafy plant right before his eyes.

Sprout hadn't known that Thordon had faerie magic; he let out a small gasp.

"How dare you intrude on me here!" Thordon shouted.

"Sorry, Thordon. I just wanted to let you know that the chocolates are all in storage and to see if you needed anything."

Thordon pointed at Eguin. "What I need is for this dragon to eat. Ever since those faeries showed up, he has refused every bit of chocolate offered."

Sprout looked over the dragon. He had seen Eguin several times, but his magnificence still took Sprout's breath away. He loved the way the light shimmered off the dragon's silver wings. And for such an enormous beast, Eguin had never evoked fear in him. Sprout could see sadness in his eyes today, though. The dragon was definitely not well. "Perhaps Veena can help," Sprout suggested.

"Bring her to me immediately. We don't have time to waste."

Sprout ran out the door, down the corridor, and exited the cavern. He ran past Gus and Bean, who shouted at him, "Where are you going in such a hurry, Sprout?"

"To get Veena for Thordon," he shouted back. He kept on running out of Eerie Hollow and didn't stop until Saizia was in sight. He realized he had no idea how he was going to get to Veena. *I can't just walk into the palace and ask for her,* he thought. *What am I going to do?* He had leaned against a tree trunk to think for a moment when he felt something hard hit him in the ear. He looked up, thinking something must have fallen off the tree, and he got hit again in the left shoulder. He turned around and saw Veena ready to throw another pebble. She quickly put her finger up to her mouth to shush him before he could speak.

Veena pretended to be picking herbs and berries while making her way closer to Sprout. When she reached the tree where he was hiding, she asked, "What are you doing here?"

"Thordon sent me to fetch you right away."

"In Saizia? Has he lost his mind?"

"I couldn't say."

"Never mind that. I will be right there, but I can't be seen with you, so go on ahead."

Sprout returned and waited for Veena just inside Eerie Hollow.

He showed himself to her, once she was close enough. "I couldn't return without you," he said in explanation.

She jumped at the sound of his voice. "Well, you didn't have to jump out at me like that."

"Sorry. We better get to Eguin's cavern." He pointed the way, and they headed off in that direction.

Sprout could hear angry voices as they were walking down the corridor to the cavern. He knocked on the door and then cautiously opened it. The voices were coming from Gus and Thordon—mostly Thordon.

"It's about time, Veena!" Thordon shouted.

"What do you want with me, Thordon?" Veena asked, clearly annoyed.

"We have to do the spell now whether or not the dragon is ready. The faeries have demanded his return to Ellyngshyme, and I won't get the chance again." Thordon sounded desperate.

"It's risky, and I'm not certain it will work."

"No matter. Do it anyway."

Veena sighed. "Very well, but I did warn you. Have you charmed the seed to grow already?"

"Yes, I just finished enchanting the blooms to open. It's over there." He pointed to the other side of the cavern.

Veena walked over to the small cacao tree and harvested a handful of the pink spiderlike blossoms growing on its branches. Then she headed straight for Eguin and put her empty hand on the dragon's face to gain his trust. With her other hand, she waved the blossoms under Eguin's nose. He sniffed them then opened his jaws. Veena fed the flowers to the dragon. Thordon then came closer to them.

"You'll need to take off your robes," Veena said to him.

Thordon hesitated for a moment but then slowly pulled them off his hunched back.

Sprout stared silently, curious as to what was hidden under his robes. One severely deformed wing, followed by another, was revealed when Thordon's robes hit the floor. They were a dull gray and misshapen. It was not clear to Sprout, but this deformity had prevented Thordon from being faerie or elf.

Thordon stepped forward and grasped Veena's outstretched hand. He placed his left hand on the other side of the dragon's scales to mimic Veena. Eguin's purple scales began to glow, starting from his head and running one by one down to his tail. Veena chanted softly, and Eguin closed his eyes and bowed his head, as if to draw all of his magic to the surface. A golden ball of glittering light formed in the center of the three of them and then began to swirl around Thordon, from head to toe and back up again until he was completely enveloped in golden light.

Veena chanted louder, holding Thordon's hand tightly so he wouldn't let go and break the spell. Sprout could see Thordon's silhouette within the circle of light, moving and transforming. As the light was fading away, it started to change from glittering gold to black smoke that circled around and around Thordon. Sprout had no idea what was supposed to happen, but the fear in Veena's faced showed that something was not right.

Thordon's deformed wings began to untangle and grow. They changed from dull gray to a brilliant sapphire blue. They were faerie wings but dark and not as delicate as the wings on other faeries. Thordon dropped to the ground in a heap. The light and smoke all dissipated.

Veena let go of the dragon and knelt down to see if Thordon was still alive. She brushed his hair from his face and revealed his now-pointed faerie ears. He lifted his head and looked at her with his now obsidian-black eyes.

He whispered, "Did it work? Am I a faerie?"

"It appears so. Do you feel all right? Thordon?"

He dropped his head, unconscious.

Veena stood up and turned to the elves. "I must get back to the palace before anyone notices I'm gone. Sprout, you'll have to look after Thordon, and give Eguin some chocolate when he wakes up."

Sprout was wide-eyed and confused. "Wha-what hap-hap-happened to Thor-Thordon?" he stammered.

"He wanted to be a full faerie. Now he is. I must go." She walked out the door and disappeared down the corridor.

Sprout stared in shock at the newly transformed Thordon but quickly enlisted Gus and Bean for assistance. Together, they transferred Thordon to his chambers and then tended to the dragon.

CHAPTER 15

Changes

äria had decided to find a quiet place away from the palace to sit with Avery, somewhere that lacked gawking faeries and guards. They hunkered down in the old hollowed-out tree by the meadow where they used to hide as young faerielings.

"I remember this place being so much bigger the last time we were here, Avery," Zäria said, while looking around the tree.

"Well, we were a lot smaller then, and so was our world."

"Amazing how much seems to have changed."

"Yeah, just last week you were just an orphaned faerie, and now you're a royal princess." He grinned at Zäria.

"Watch it, Avery, or I'll have you thrown in the dungeon for mocking me." She laughed at the thought.

Avery bowed to her and said in a dramatic tone, "My deepest apologies, Your Majesty." He could barely contain his laughter. "Hey, do you think the palace has a real dungeon?"

"I don't know, but if it does, you'll be the first to take a tour." She couldn't hold her serious expression for too long. Relaxed now, she smiled at Avery and took a seat on the dandelion blossom she used as a cushion.

Avery lay on an oak leaf, propping his head on his right hand. "Just like when we were kids," he said with a sigh.

"What do you think I should do, Avery?"

"About what?"

"Should I move into the palace in Saizia, or go to Ellyngshyme?"

"That's a lot to think about."

"I know, and with so much going on, I haven't had time to take it all in. I'm a *princess*! Can you believe it?"

"No, but it does explain why you are so bossy."

"Avery Lightfoot!" Zäria exclaimed as she pushed him over and held him down. They both laughed so hard that it was easy for Avery to grab hold of Zäria's waist and flip her over. As he did, something suddenly came over him, and he kissed her.

Zäria was shocked at first but then kissed him back. She had never kissed any faerie, but it seemed so natural with Avery, and all her troubles melted away when his lips touched hers.

When they pulled apart and slowly opened their eyes, both had blushing cheeks. Avery helped Zäria sit up and brushed the loose strands of hair away from her face.

Zäria suddenly blurted out, "Do that again! Kiss me."

Avery raised an eyebrow and then leaned in to kiss her again, entwining their fingers together.

Zäria's cheeks were still flushed. She looked at him with adoration and said, "I thought you never would, no matter how many hints I've given you. You really are hard-headed Avery." She giggled and smiled at him.

They sat in awkward silence for a few moments, and then Avery finally spoke. "Well, now that it's allowed, do you want to go to Eerie Hollow?"

Zäria looked shocked. "Why would I ever want to go back there?"

"So are you all done having adventures then?" he teased.

"For the time being, I think I'd like to enjoy where I am … and who I'm with." She leaned in and kissed Avery again.

He put his arm around her shoulders, and she nuzzled up against him with her head resting on his chest.

"I think you should stay in Saizia," Avery said. "I want you to stay here and not go to Ellyngshyme, I mean."

"So you think I should move into the palace with Yamani?"

"I think you would be safer there than at your place, especially once everyone knows who your parents are."

Zäria looked up at him. "Avery, does it bother you that Thordon is my father?"

"Of course not. That doesn't change who you are at all. You will always be Zäria to me, even when they put that crown on your head." He squeezed her a bit tighter in his arms.

Zäria smiled contently. "I think we should let Yamani know I've made my decision to move into the palace."

"Let's not rush. We've been in that palace quite a bit lately."

"Might as well get used to it. I'm a princess now."

"You've always been a princess, Zäria."

Zäria blushed. "Well, now I have to act like it."

Avery stood up and pulled Zäria by her hands to help her up. He then bowed to her. "Your Majesty, shall I escort you to your palace?"

She giggled at his silliness and then took his hand. "Avery, something else has been weighing on my mind. I've been afraid to tell you, but now that we are alone ..."

Avery looked worried. "What is it, Zär? You can tell me anything. You know that."

"I think I've started getting my faerie magic," she said cautiously and then waited for his reaction.

"Already? Wow! What can you do?"

Zäria was surprised that Avery seemed excited for her. She relaxed a bit and told him all about the visions and how she telekinetically had pushed that witch. They talked about it for hours. After watching the sunset together, Zäria suggested they go talk to Yamani. As they exited the tree, Zäria looked back at their childhood hiding place and sighed.

Then they walked in the direction of the palace—but they took the long way.

Thordon lay motionless on his bed, where the elves had placed him.

Sprout asked Gus, "Do you think he is only sleeping?"

"I hope so. I'm not sure what would become of Eerie Hollow if Thordon never woke," Gus replied.

Thordon opened his eyes. He was surprised to see the elves at the foot of his bed. "Why are you in my quarters, gawking at me? Don't you have work to do?"

"We brought you here after you collapsed," Gus answered.

"Collapsed? Whatever are you going on about, Gus?" Thordon asked angrily.

"You collapsed after Veena did that spell that changed you. Perhaps you were just tired."

"Changed me?" He quickly jumped to his feet. "What happened to my wings?"

"They look fine to me," said Bean.

"Perhaps you should take a look in the mirror, Thordon," Gus suggested.

Thordon walked over to the mirror. His appearance took him by surprise. His face had changed so much. He looked like a faerie, except for his dark, obsidian eyes. His wings were magnificent. He stretched them out and flapped them a few times. He wondered if he could fly. He flapped his wings hard and shot up in the air. It wasn't the most graceful flight but not bad for the first go. His landing was a bit abrupt. As he collected himself, a sinister grin formed on his face, and he admired his new fae physique in the mirror. He turned to the elves. "Prepare the dragon to leave."

"Sire, Eguin may not be in the best shape for travel," Gus said.

"What is wrong with Eguin?" Thordon asked.

Gus shrugged, "Possibly nothing, but he also collapsed when you did, sire, and I have yet to return to his cavern to check on him."

"Then why are you fools still here?" he yelled. "There is nothing wrong with me. Get down there and prepare that dragon to leave. I have business to attend to immediately."

Once the meddlesome elves were out of sight, Thordon tested his wings a bit more. He fluttered them in front of the mirror, admiring how perfect they were. He had always longed to have beautiful, working faerie wings, and now he finally had them. He laughed maniacally and flapped his wings hard. He flew in circles and loops, swooping through his room and down the corridors. He spread out his wings and slowly descended to the ground, just outside Eguin's cavern.

"Why are you all standing around, and this dragon is not ready to depart?" Thordon bellowed as he walked into the cavern. The dwarfs were awestruck at seeing Thordon in his new faerish form. He no longer hid his wings under his robes. They were stretched out, in all their sapphire glory, behind him. "Back to work, dwarfs," he ordered. He then directed his attention to the elves. "Prepare yourselves; you are coming along."

The elves nodded and headed out of the cavern to collect their things.

Thordon walked over to Eguin. He leaned near and said, "You did well, dragon. Time to send you home." Then he put his hand on the dragon's chest.

Instantly, Eguin awoke and clasped Thordon's arms in his talons. The magic had connected them, and Thordon felt it as soon as he touched the dragon. He did not attempt to free himself. They just looked each other in the eyes for a few moments before Eguin released Thordon's arms.

Thordon barked at the dwarfs, "Once he is ready, bring the dragon to me outside." Then he quickly exited the cavern.

CHAPTER 16

Invasion

Yamani was surprised to see that Zäria had returned to the palace so soon. "Zäria, I'm so glad you and Avery you're here. Please have a seat." She gestured to the chairs beside her throne. The queen waited as the two fae sat down. "Have you given my offer any thought, dear?" she asked Zäria.

"Yes, that is why we have come. We decided ... I mean, I decided that it might be best for me to live in your palace here in Saizia."

Yamani clapped her hands with excitement. "Oh, that is wonderful. I will have your room set up for you and make you as comfortable as possible. You may have the guards bring your personal belongings to help you feel at home here." She then reached over and placed a hand on Avery's arm. "You are welcome at the palace any time, Avery. I would never keep Zäria's best friend from her."

"I have to admit, Your Majesty, that it is kind of cool to be best friends with a real princess." Avery laughed. Yamani and Zäria joined him.

One of Yamani's guards entered the room. "Excuse me, Your Majesty. Holvar wishes to see you. He has Veena with him."

"Bring them in at once." Yamani watched as the doors opened, and Holvar entered the room, with Veena bound to his side. Holvar bowed and then pushed Veena down to her knees before Yamani.

"Holvar, I see you have found our missing sorceress. Where did you find her?" inquired the queen.

"Your Majesty, she was fleeing Eerie Hollow when I caught her," he replied.

Yamani glared at Veena disapprovingly. "You have been found poking about in places you don't belong, Veena. What is your business in Eerie Hollow?"

Veena held her head down. "I have been helping Thordon."

"Helping him with what, exactly?" Yamani asked angrily.

"Thordon has been preparing the dragon to perform a spell, and he coerced me to assist him."

"Does this have anything to do with that seed he forced Zäria and Avery to collect?"

"Yes, it—"

"Sorry to barge in, Your Majesty," a guard interrupted. Yamani's attention quickly turned to the guard who had burst through the doors. He quickly bowed to the queen. "Someone is approaching the palace gates, accompanied by those elves and a large dragon."

Yamani rose from her throne. "It must be Thordon. Place all guards on full alert. Bring him to me, and keep the dragon outside the gates."

The guard nodded and left the room.

Yamani grabbed Zäria's hand and pulled her to her feet. "Avery, take Zäria and keep hidden behind these curtains," she directed. She reached behind her throne, swept the curtains aside, and ushered them in. "I do not want Thordon to know you are here. No matter what happens, do not reveal yourselves." Yamani straightened out the curtains hiding the young fae and made certain they could not be seen. She saw that Holvar had his sword drawn. "Prepare yourself, Holvar," she advised and awaited Thordon's arrival.

Zäria pulled the curtains back just enough to see four guards escorting Thordon and his elves into the throne room. She did a double-take when she saw Thordon and gasped in shock at his faerish appearance. It was just like her vision—he had magnificent blue wings—but it was his eyes that filled her heart with distrust. They were so black, cold, and empty.

"Thordon, what have you done to yourself?" Yamani asked. Her voice cracked as she spoke.

I wish I could see Yamani's face, Zäria thought.

Thordon bowed without fanfare and replied, "Yamani, Your Majesty, I see you've noticed my new look. Do you like it?" He proudly spread his wings and turned in a complete circle to show them to her.

"Well, it definitely took me by surprise. Is this why you were so obsessed with obtaining that seed?" the queen asked.

"Yes, it provided the final ingredient needed to cast the transformation spell—the cocoa blossoms."

Yamani asked him the question Zäria was just thinking. "We just gave you that seed. How did you get cocoa blossoms from it already, Thordon?"

"Have you really forgotten? The one gift of faerie magic I was given was the ability to make things grow." He produced a red rose in his hand and placed it in Yamani's lap.

For the first time, Zäria saw the charm her mother must have seen in him those many years ago.

"I spent years trying to find a way to break that stupid pact," Thordon said. "Perhaps my desire to win you back turned into an obsession to become a full faerie. I finally found the formula to transform myself, but I needed more magic than a half elf possessed. So I stole the dwarfs' dragon and built up his magical powers. Then I forced your sorceress to help me." He pointed at Veena, who was still on the ground, bound to the queen's guard. "Then after all that time and effort to get all I needed to perform the spell, the pact was abolished—right after I got the final ingredient. It didn't matter anymore. I decided to go through with it anyway, and here I am. Just look at my perfect wings, Yamani." He spread his wings out again and took flight, twirling in a few dramatic circles.

"That is quite enough, Thordon. We don't fly inside the palace. It's dangerous and quite rude at that," Yamani scolded.

"Very well. I apologize. I do enjoy being able to fly. It is a glorious feeling." He landed in front of the queen and kneeled before her. "Dear Queen Yamani, now that we are not so different, and it is not forbidden, would you reclaim me as your husband and join our kingdoms?"

Zäria was shocked at the proposal. She waited for Yamani's response, but there was a long silence.

"Don't keep me waiting for an answer, my queen. I've already waited so long for this moment."

"Thordon, it's true that I loved you once, but you can't possibly think that after all this time and all that has happened that I would be able to accept your offer at a moment's notice. I appreciate the gesture of going as far as changing yourself into a faerie, but I am obliged to humbly decline. I am so sorry, Thordon."

Zäria could see Thordon glare at the queen with his obsidian eyes, as if trying to set her on fire. He stood up slowly and snarled, "You dare turn me down. I have done nothing to deserve the rejection you and your family have placed upon me. Everything and everyone I have ever loved have been taken from me. You will pay!" He looked around the room and shouted, "You will *all pay*! I'm ashamed that I wanted to be a faerie so badly."

Avery put his arm around Zäria and pulled her closer to him. She wanted to run to her mother's aid, but she heeded her orders to stay hidden. Instead, she watched helplessly from the comfort of Avery's arms as the guards, with swords drawn, surrounded Thordon and the elves.

Thordon laughed maniacally. "You think you can stop me now? I not only have faerie magic, but I have dragon magic as well."

Zäria was horrified as all the guards fell to the ground, pushed by an invisible force thrown at them from Thordon's hands. More guards stormed into the room, and he blocked them from getting near him with the same invisible force.

In a panic, Zäria whispered to Avery, "That was the telekinetic faerie magic that I used on that witch, but Thordon needed dragon magic to do it."

"Wow, that is really powerful faerie magic. Can you use it now?"

"I'm not sure how, and I don't know if I could attack my own father Avery."

Just then Yamani rose from her throne and yelled, "Do something, Veena!"

Zäria peered through the curtains and saw Veena hold her arm up to the queen—her shackles prevented her from using magic. Holvar removed the shackles and released her. Veena threw all the magic she had at Thordon, but the spells just bounced off him without a trace of harm. It seemed to only make Thordon angrier. He stomped toward Veena with hands out and threw her across the room. She hit her head so hard against the stone wall that she collapsed to the floor with blood running down her face. Gus ran to her and cradled her head in his arms, wiping the blood on his sleeve.

"Zär, you have to try your magic," Avery urged, but Zäria was too scared to move. She watched, paralyzed, as Thordon turned his attention back to the queen.

He walked up the steps to her throne. Yamani stood strong. Once he was face-to-face with her, he leaned in and kissed her on the lips. Yamani angrily pushed him away in disgust. He stumbled just enough that his magic force field wavered. The guards were able to push their way through, but Thordon took flight and fled the room before they could reach him.

Zäria could hear the panicked screams of the faeries of Saizia outside the gates, and she felt guilty for being too scared to defend them. She pulled herself from Avery's grip and ran out from behind the curtains. She slipped past Yamani and out through the doors. She could hear Yamani and Avery yelling for her to stop as they chased her, but she didn't stop running until she was just outside the palace doors—and she saw Thordon just ahead of her. Avery and Yamani had caught up to her just as Thordon lit a torch and screamed at Eguin, "Destroy everything, dragon!"

Horror-stricken, Zäria witnessed Thordon set faerie structures on fire. Eguin obeyed Thordon's command and crushed everything in sight. Faeries ran in every direction, screaming, trying to shelter each other.

Zäria yelled at a family of faeries to watch out for the dragon. She instinctively threw her hands out toward them, and her faerie magic pushed them out of the way before Eguin's foot crashed down where they had stood. The magic temporarily stunned Zäria, and then she realized she needed to continue using it to save Saizia. She magically pushed the dragon away from the faerie houses to stop him from destroying them, threw water on the fires Thordon had started, and slammed the palace gates shut to protect Yamani.

Zäria's eyesight got hazy as she watched Thordon and Eguin fly off in the distance, and then she dropped to the ground from exhaustion.

Avery gathered her in his arms. "Are you okay?" he shouted. "Zär, answer me!"

She shook her head to snap herself out of her daze. She wasn't sure if this was real or a horrid nightmare. She saw the fear on Avery's and Yamani's faces as they hovered over her. She grasped Avery's arms as he pulled her to her feet.

Zäria looked around her and was devastated by the destruction before her. Then the realization that she had revealed her faerie magic to Yamani and Avery hit her. She turned to Yamani. "I'm sorry I disobeyed and chased after Thordon. I just couldn't hide while he destroyed Saizia."

Yamani brushed Zäria's hair from her face and touched her cheek softly. "I am glad you did, Zäria. You saved much of Saizia from being destroyed and protected your fellow fae. I couldn't be more proud of you, dear."

Zäria beamed. "Really? I was so scared to use my faerie magic."

"You have a gift with that kind of faerie magic, Zäria. Use it wisely. I need to tend to the kingdom. Avery take Zäria inside to rest."

Zäria took Avery's arm and allowed him to lead her back into the palace. She felt like all her energy had been drained from her body.

Once inside, Avery set her down in the first chair he could find. "Here you are, Zäria. Sit for a bit and catch your breath." He sat down next to her and wrapped his arm around her so she could rest her head on his shoulder. He stroked her soft blonde hair. "That magic of yours was pretty awesome to watch, Zär. You fought a dragon!"

"I didn't fight a dragon. Don't exaggerate, Avery."

He smiled. "I can always count on you to set me straight, even in your current state. So okay, you pushed a dragon, and you protected Saizia. You're a hero."

Zäria lifted her head from his shoulder. "I didn't know what I was doing, and I don't feel very heroic."

Avery squeezed her tight. "Well, you're *my* hero." He kissed her on the cheek. He was startled by Yamani as she came back into the palace.

"Avery, bring Zäria to the potions room. We must get a faerie stone right away."

Avery scooped Zäria from the chair and carried her as he followed Yamani to the potions room. He had a hard time keeping up with her as she quickly made her way through the winding corridors and was relieved to set Zäria down once they were inside the potions room.

Yamani searched the room, dumping out baskets and opening drawers. "I know there's one around here somewhere," Yamani muttered. She suddenly stopped digging through a basket and held up a sparkling blue stone. "Aha! Veena's faerie stone." Yamani dropped it into Avery's open hand. "This is a faerie stone," she explained. "Hold it tight in one hand and hold Zäria tight in the other. Think hard that you need help from the faerie sanctuary, and you will be teleported there. Warn the king and queen that Ellyngshyme may be in danger."

"Yes, Your Majesty," Avery said.

"I'm counting on you to take care of Zäria."

"Of course," Avery replied. He then followed the queen's instructions on how to use the faerie stone. He closed his eyes and tightened his grip on the faerie stone and on Zäria.

CHAPTER 17

Sanctuary

t first it didn't feel like anything had happened at all, but when Avery opened his eyes, he was inside the faerie sanctuary, still holding Zäria, and Yamani was gone.

Fynn came running to them. "Oh, young fae! You're back. Is everything all right? You used a faerie stone to get here."

Zäria couldn't speak, so Avery responded, "Actually, Fynn, we need to talk to the king and queen right away. Something has happened in Saizia, and we need help."

"Well, you came to the right place. I will have Ogg escort you to the throne room, and I'll go fetch you something to eat. You both look pale." She ran off to the kitchen, leaving them alone in the room—until in walked a familiar bearded gnome.

"Ogg, we sure are glad to see you!" Avery exclaimed.

"Likewise. Come, young fae. Fynn says you need to see the king and queen straightaway." He gestured for them to follow him down the corridor. When they reached the throne room, it was empty. "Please wait here while I announce your arrival. I will be back shortly." Ogg quickly left the room.

As he was leaving, two royal guards entered the room and flanked the door. Avery felt better not being left alone. He knew they'd be safe here, but he didn't know his way around the sanctuary without an escort.

Queen Xandria came in first, running straight to Zäria and wrapping her arms around her. "Zäria, what happened?"

"Thordon is destroying Saizia!" Zäria cried. "He had Eguin with him, and they were smashing homes, gardens, the faerie school—everything."

King Byron had entered the room and asked, "And Yamani?"

"Yamani is safe," Avery replied. "She sent us here to warn you that Thordon may be on his way here next."

"Dear me, this is not going the way we had hoped," the queen admitted. "Oggbotham, advise Rorik to assemble his most trusted guards and to join us immediately," the king ordered.

Ogg nodded, turned on his heel, and left the room.

Avery stood with Zäria as the king and queen seated themselves on their thrones. Avery helped Zäria into a chair next to them and took a seat on the step at Zäria's feet while they awaited the guards. He stood up quickly when Rorik and the other guards entered the room. He still felt a bit intimidated by them. The guards came to a stop in front of the king and queen and bowed to them.

Rorik addressed the king. "Your Majesty, I understand there is an urgent matter at hand. How can my guards assist?"

"Thordon has attacked the kingdom of Saizia, with Eguin's help," the king said.

Rorik clenched his fists at the mention of Eguin's name. "How dare that miserable half elf turn our dragon against us!" he exclaimed angrily.

Zäria timidly interrupted. "There's something else you should know. I don't think he is half elf anymore."

"What do you mean, Zäria?" asked the queen.

"He looked different. I mean, he was still dark, but now his eyes are black as night, and he has wings—real faerie wings."

Queen Xandria turned to one of her attendants and ordered her to bring Ambrosia and Goran immediately.

King Byron shook his head. "Rorik, we fear that Thordon may be headed to Ellyngshyme next. We must strengthen all of our defenses while being available to take in all the faeries in Saizia who are in need of sanctuary."

Rorik nodded in agreement. "May I suggest we briefly adjourn this meeting to reinforce the perimeter of Ellyngshyme? We can then safely assemble to form a plan of attack against Thordon."

"Very well, Rorik. We will assemble here in one hour's time."

Just as Rorik bowed to the king and directed his troop out of the throne room, Ambrosia and Goran walked in.

Queen Xandria explained, "Ambrosia, there seems to be an issue in Saizia. Thordon has somehow transformed into a faerie and used Eguin attack the kingdom."

Ambrosia shook her head and started pacing back and forth, mumbling angrily to herself. "I knew we shouldn't have handed that seed over to Thordon. He must have used the dragon's magic and the cocoa seed somehow to turn himself into a faerie. It would have formed a temporary connection between the two, and Eguin would have been forced to obey him." Ambrosia raised an eyebrow. "That takes a lot of magic and a lot of knowledge of magic. Thordon possesses neither. He must have had help from a sorceress."

"Mother, are you implying that our Veena had something to do with this?" gasped Goran.

Ambrosia put her hand on his shoulder. "It's deductive reasoning, dear. If it wasn't you or I, it had to be her."

"Veena was helping Thordon," Zäria interjected. "Queen Yamani had suspected this and ordered a guard to follow her. She was found leaving Eerie Hollow and was brought to Yamani, where she confessed just before the attack."

Avery added, "Ambrosia, she tried to stop Thordon, but he attacked her and knocked her unconscious. We did not get a chance to check on her condition before we left Saizia."

"We cannot allow Thordon to have access to the immeasurable magical power that Eguin possesses" Ambrosia insisted. "Thordon built up the dragon's power with all that chocolate he was feeding him, and now they share a magical bond. Our forces will be no match against them if Thordon learns how to harness that magic. We need to remove all the magical forces to which Thordon has access. He used Veena to cast the charm to turn him into a faerie. I do not know how else she has helped Thordon, but we cannot take a chance of allowing him to strengthen his magical defenses. We must get Eguin and Veena to Ellyngshyme as soon as possible."

"Very sensible idea," said King Byron. "We must act quickly. I will send Rorik and his guards immediately."

CHAPTER 18

Rescue

Rorik and his guards arrived at the palace gate in Saizia, which was securely locked. He looked around to assess the damage. Faerie doors had been broken off hinges and were on the ground, roofs had caved in or were shredded apart, and even the flower gardens had been trampled. There were no faeries in sight.

One of the guards said to Rorik, "It's such a shame to see Saizia in ruin." The others nodded in agreement.

Rorik was recognized in Saizia as a guard of Ellyngshyme, and so his troop was let in. Once inside the palace, Rorik found this was where all the faeries of Saizia had taken refuge.

One of Yamani's guards said to Rorik, "The faeries have kept busy with fixing up the palace—the inside was in a similar condition as the outside. Yamani told them they could go to the sanctuary, but most chose to stay. Saizia is very loyal to Yamani."

"And Yamani—she was unharmed?" asked Rorik.

"See for yourself," the guard said, pointing to the door.

Rorik opened the door to the throne room to find Queen Yamani pacing back and forth as several faeries were cleaning and replacing broken and damaged décor.

The guards all took a knee and bowed to the queen.

"You may rise," said the queen. "Rorik, you may tell my parents that I appreciate the gesture, but Saizia is not in need of sanctuary protection."

"Your Majesty, it was not their intention to imply that Saizia is incapable of protecting its kingdom," Rorik responded. "I apologize on behalf of Ellyngshyme if you have been offended by our presence. King Byron ordered us to collect Veena so Ambrosia can nurse her back to health and keep her from Thordon's grasp."

"Unfortunately, Veena was a casualty of Thordon's wrath. The apothecaries were unable to save her. I have not been able to get word to Ambrosia yet."

"That is sad news indeed. I would deliver the message to Ambrosia personally, but we have orders to go to Eerie Hollow and seize Eguin from Thordon."

Yamani gasped. "With so few guards? That is a reckless mission."

"Ellyngshymé was only willing to spare a few guards so as to not leave the sanctuary vulnerable to attack. We fear Thordon's next move will be to infiltrate the sanctuary."

"Perhaps you should take some of my guards with you, Rorik," Yamani suggested.

"Your Majesty, I must respectfully decline your offer. Saizia requires the protection of your guards more than we do. King Byron sent us to check on your health and the safety of your people. We can see you are well and have your people well protected inside the palace. If you can see to it that Veena is sent to Ellyngshyme to be buried with her mother, then our work here is done."

"I understand. Do be careful—all of you. Thordon is unpredictable and dangerous," warned the queen.

"I agree." Rorik bowed. "We bid you farewell, Your Highness." He turned on his heels and marched out of the palace to begin the journey to his troop's next destination.

Yamani and one of her ladies-in-waiting proceeded to Veena's chambers.

As they arrived, the apothecary was just leaving and passed them in the hall.

Yamani stopped him. "Excuse me ..."

Startled, he dropped the potion bottles he was carrying, and they shattered on the floor. "Oh, I'm sorry, Your Highness. I'm so clumsy these days," he said as he tried to clean up his mess without much success.

"It's quite all right, Ezri. I didn't mean to startle you," said Yamani.

Ezri stood up and wiped his hands on his cloak haphazardly and then bowed deeply to Yamani. "Your Majesty, my deepest sympathy. I'm so sorry I couldn't save Veena. I tried every potion I had. Thordon's magic is powerful."

"I understand, Ezri. I am confident you did your very best. We need to prepare her to be moved to Ellyngshyme to be with her family."

"Yes, of course," Ezri replied. "The elf stayed with her—Gus, I believe."

"Thank you, Ezri. I will see to him. You may continue on to wherever you were headed before I stopped you."

"If I can only remember where that was. Thank you, Your Majesty." Ezri bowed graciously and then hurried off down the hall.

Yamani and her attendant walked into the room. Veena was in her bed with bandages on her head and arms. She looked as though she was asleep. Gus was sitting at her bedside, holding her hand. Tears rolled down his face.

The elf stood and bowed when Yamani entered the room. "Your Majesty, I hope you do not mind that I stayed behind with Veena."

"You are more than welcome, Gus. I can see that you cared for her," replied the queen.

His head hung down remorsefully. "I'm really sorry for what Thordon did to your kingdom."

"As I am sorry for what he did to Veena, but Thordon's actions were out of our control, I'm afraid." Yamani came closer to Veena's bed and took her hand. "Out of respect to Veena's family, I must send her to Ellyngshyme. I need someone to accompany her in order to use faerie magic. Would you mind?"

"Of course, Your Majesty. I'd be glad to."

"Very good. Hold out your hand."

Gus held out his hand, and Yamani placed a glowing purple pebble in it.

"I've never seen anything like it," he said. "It's beautiful. What is it?"

"It is a faerie stone. This is how faeries safely travel to the sanctuary from far away. Just hold it tightly in one hand, and hold Veena's hand with the other. Say that you need sanctuary in Ellyngshyme, and you will be transported instantly to safety."

Gus closed the fingers of his right hand around the stone and held Veena's hand in his left. He said clearly, "I need the sanctuary of Ellyngshyme."

There was a small wisp of purple smoke, and they were gone.

Rorik and his crew flew into Eerie Hollow as quietly as possible. They landed just outside the main cave entrance. He motioned for everyone to follow him into the cave. One by one, they silently entered the darkness. It was much too quiet, but they continued on down the corridor. Rorik started to hear voices and other noises coming from up ahead. As they grew closer, the voices became louder, but it sounded like everyone was yelling at once, and he could not make out what they were saying.

Rorik saw a flickering light dance across the floor and up the cave wall outside of an open doorway. The guards stayed close to the cave wall as they slowly moved toward the doorway. Rorik carefully inched forward to peek into the room. It was packed with fae, elves, dwarfs, and the like.

All of Eerie Hollow must be in this room, he thought. He pulled back and whispered to the others what he'd seen.

"Is Eguin in there?" Boro whispered.

"I did not see him." Rorik motioned for them to keep moving. "Don't let anyone see you."

They proceeded through the corridors and seemed to be gradually moving deeper underground. Rorik saw a blue light coming from a large cavern straight ahead of them. Even though he could not hear anyone in the room, he took precautions to not bring attention to them. As he reached the opening, he slowly looked around the corner and inside the cavern. There in the blue light sat his dragon, chained and shackled to the cave floor. It angered him to see Eguin with his head hung down, alone, and being treated like a prisoner. He stopped himself from running straight for the dragon to set him free and took a moment to look around the room for any sign of Thordon or one of his minions.

When he didn't see or hear anyone, he said to his men, "Eguin is in there, shackled to the floor!" Hurt and anger resounded in his voice. "He appears to be alone. We should act fast before anyone comes to check on him."

The guards quickly followed Rorik into the cave. The dragon perked up when he saw Rorik coming to his aid. Rorik put his hand up to warn Eguin to not make a sound. The guards began to work on the shackles to free the dragon. Once loose, Eguin spread out his massive wings and the chains noisily hit the floor before any of them could catch them.

Startled by the noise, Sprout, who had been napping in the corner, yelled out, "What are you doing?"

The guards all pulled out their weapons, ready to defend themselves and the dragon.

"Are you the fool who bound this dragon in chains?" Rorik shouted

"Of course not," replied Sprout. "Thordon shackled him and ordered me to stay here until he returned. Are you Yamani's guards? Is she okay?"

"No, we are guards of Ellyngshyme. We can assure you that Queen Yamani is well, no thanks to Thordon's betrayal," Rorik spat.

Sprout looked at the floor in shame. "I wasn't expecting any of this to happen. I should have stayed in Saizia with Gus, but I wanted to know what Thordon was going to do next. I can't bear to see those faeries get hurt." He looked up at Eguin and then at Rorik. "I'm not going to stop you from taking the dragon. Please take me with you. If Thordon returns and sees I've let the dragon escape, it will be my life."

Rorik scowled at him. "We can't risk taking you to Ellyngshyme. I don't think you have the means to stop us from taking our dragon either. The most I can do for you, in case you mean what you say, is this ..." He quickly threw up his fist, hit Sprout square in the jaw, and sent him flying to the ground, unconscious. Rorik looked down at him. "Now Thordon will think you were overpowered." Rorik scanned the room. "Now to find a way out. We can't sneak down those corridors with a dragon."

Rorik noticed Eguin looking upward; he followed the dragon's gaze to find the top of the cave was open to the sky. *That must have been why Eguin was shackled,* he thought, *to keep him from flying away.*

"Do you remember the way to the sanctuary, Eguin?" he asked. Eguin nodded his head in response.

Rorik advised his men, "Eguin can fly out of here, but he cannot carry us in his condition. We will have to use the faerie stone to get us back to Ellyngshyme." He nodded to Eguin, and the dragon took flight.

Eguin was extremely out of shape from eating all the chocolates and the lack of training, so it took him a few moments to find his bearings. He flapped his wings in slow, deep strides to push himself up through the opening in the cavern.

The guards then huddled together as Rorik pulled out the glowing faerie stone. They all held tightly to him.

Just then, Thordon came storming in. "What have you done with my dragon?" he shouted.

But it was too late; they disappeared in a puff of smoke.

When they reappeared, they were just outside the tree of the sanctuary. Boro looked around, confused. "Why are we outside?"

"That is a good question, Boro. Looks like we're not the only ones," Rorik said, nodding toward Gus and the lifeless Veena.

"Please don't hurt me," begged Gus. "Queen Yamani told me to make sure she gets to Ellyngshyme."

"You are in the right place. We are the guards of Ellyngshyme, and we sent for Veena to come. How did you get here?"

"Queen Yamani gave me a faerie stone to send us here with faerie magic," Gus said.

"It should have taken you inside. It should have taken all of us inside." Rorik went up to the tree and hit it with his hand, looking for the door. Gus watched him, unsure of what to say. Suddenly, Rorik was thrown from the tree by an invisible force. He fell to the ground a few feet from Gus and Veena. Before Rorik could get back on his feet, a bright white light appeared from the side of the tree. Everyone averted their eyes from the glare.

Rorik saw a silhouette of a guard then felt the point of a spear at his throat. When the light dimmed a bit, it took a moment for Rorik's eyes to focus and he realized the guard was Drovak.

"Drovak, can't you see who we are? What is going on? Why are we locked out of Ellyngshyme?" Rorik demanded.

Drovak quickly withdrew his spear. "My apologies, sir." Drovak extended an arm to assist Rorik to his feet. Rorik took it reluctantly. "Ambrosia and Goran increased the protection charms around the sanctuary so no one can teleport directly inside. Somehow, you set off the intrusion alarms."

"Do the king and queen know about this?" Rorik asked gruffly.

"Let's get you all inside, and you can discuss your complaints with them directly," Drovak said. He nodded toward Veena, lying on the ground. "Is that Ambrosia's granddaughter?"

"Yes, it is. Thordon killed her," Rorik said solemnly.

Drovak picked up Veena and carried her through the door of the sanctuary. Gus followed closely behind them. Rorik and the guards looked around and then entered.

Once inside, Drovak said over his shoulder to Rorik, "I'm going to take Veena to Ambrosia. You can report to the king and queen in the study." Gus cleared his throat to get Drovak's attention. "You can come with me, elf."

Gus followed Drovak, leaving Rorik and his men behind.

"Now that everyone has made it inside, I'm going to go out to look for Eguin," Rorik told his men. "Make sure to let the king and queen know not to lock me out again." The men nodded.

Once Rorik was outside, it didn't take long to find the dragon. Eguin was lying on the ground, visibly weak, not far from the sanctuary. Rorik ran to him. "Eguin, you are out of shape, but you made it. Excellent job, dragon." He petted the dragon on the head and then emptied the contents of his water pouch into Eguin's mouth. "I hope the protection shields are down. The only way you are getting inside is by teleporting into the dragon chamber." He held the faerie stone in one hand and grabbed the dragon with the other.

At first Rorik thought it had worked, but when he opened his eyes, he realized they had only moved closer to the sanctuary but were still outside. "Looks like they haven't finished yet." He waited a few more minutes and tried again, but nothing happened at all. They didn't even move. "I think we are going to be stuck outside for a while, Eguin."

Rorik thought he saw something in the distance. He stood up to get a better look. It appeared to be a faerie flying toward him. *Perhaps it's a faerie from Saizia,* he thought. He waited for the faerie to get closer to see if he recognized who it was. When he realized it was Thordon, he quickly ran back to Eguin and pulled out the faerie stone, but it slipped from his fingers and fell into the grass. Rorik frantically searched the grass for the stone. Once he found it, he grabbed hold of the dragon, held the stone tight, and tried to leap once again.

This time there was the familiar puff of purple smoke.

When Rorik opened his eyes, he was inside the dragon chamber … but Eguin was nowhere to be seen. He must have lost his grip on the dragon somehow.

"Good; you made it inside," said Boro as he walked into the room. "It took a bit longer than we expected to get Ambrosia and Goran to take down the protection charms. Where did you put the dragon?"

"Somehow, he didn't leap with me; worse, Thordon is here."

"Thordon found the sanctuary?" Boro asked, surprised.

Rorik nodded. "We need to alert the king, and prepare to fight."

CHAPTER 19

Retribution

äria and Avery were with the king and queen in their study when Rorik and Boro entered the room. Boro had already announced their safe arrival, so Zäria assumed that they were coming to report on the dragon.

"Rorik, did you manage to get the dragon inside safely?" King Byron asked.

"He didn't make it inside, and to make matters worse, Thordon has found the sanctuary. I saw him fly in just as I used the faerie stone to bring in Eguin. I'm not sure why the dragon did not leap with me."

Zäria felt her heart beat faster, just knowing that Thordon was here.

King Byron stood up. "Send every available guard outside to fight, and gather all the faeries who possess magic. We need to rely on all of our resources to protect Ellyngshyme."

"Come on, Boro. Let's get the guards prepared to fight," Rorik ordered.

"I'd better find my mother and start gathering the magical fae," Goran said. He bowed and left the room.

Avery put his hand on Zäria's, and suddenly she had another vision …

Avery was on the ground. He wasn't moving. Panic coursed through her veins. She was leaning over him, screaming. She looked up to see Thordon flying straight at her.

As soon as the vision faded, she looked at Avery to make sure he was unharmed.

Zäria suddenly had a change of heart about using her magic against Thordon. She had to get outside, but she knew that the king and queen would never allow it. "Avery," she said quietly, "I need to speak to Ambrosia. I'll be right back."

While everyone was involved in a heated conversation about Thordon, she slipped out the door unnoticed.

She needed to get outside to prevent Thordon from getting a chance to hurt Avery. She flew straight to the sanctuary door and made it outside without a hitch. A flood of panic washed over her once she realized she was the only one outside. She had assumed the guards would already be there. *Too late to worry about that now,* she thought. *I need to find Thordon.*

Zäria silently made her way around the great tree, looking for Thordon and Eguin. Once she was halfway around, she heard Thordon's voice. She slowly peered around the edge of the tree to get a look at what was happening. Eguin was lying on the ground, and Thordon was trying to coax him to get up by offering him chocolates. It didn't seem to be working. Zäria debated whether she should attack now, while it appeared the dragon was incapacitated, or wait for the guards. She decided it might be best to observe for at least a few minutes and come up with a plan of attack.

Then she saw Thordon kick the obviously exhausted dragon in his side. He yelled at him, "Get up, you worthless, fat dragon!"

That was the last straw for Zäria. Reinforcements or not, she would teach Thordon a lesson. Adrenaline from her anger and the tinge of fear quickly built up and turned into reckless courage. She flew straight at Thordon, screaming wildly, hands outstretched. She called upon all her magic and felt it course through her body—from her toes through her wings and out the tips of her fingers. Sparks of magic shot from her hands like fire, and it traveled through the air and hit Thordon square in the chest. The blow came as a surprise to him and knocked him a good five feet away from the dragon.

Zäria did not allow him time to compose himself before she threw another bolt of magic at him and pinned him to the ground. "How dare you kick that defenseless creature while he's down!" she spat. "I should destroy you for what you did to Saizia and Veena!"

"Zäria, what has gotten into you?" Rorik yelled from behind her.

It threw off her concentration, and she lost hold of the magic that pinned Thordon down. She suddenly felt her chest burn, and the wind was knocked out of her when Thordon sent a bolt of magic at her that sent her crashing into Rorik. Rorik and two other guards pushed her back and stepped in front of her with their swords drawn.

Zäria shouted, "Rorik, your weapons are no use against Thordon's magic!" She tried to right herself but felt a hand on her arm, pulling her away. She turned around to see Avery with a very angry look on his face.

"I'll be right back," he mimicked her. "Have you lost your ever-loving mind, Zär? I have been looking everywhere for you. You could have been killed."

"Avery, you shouldn't be out here. Thordon is going to kill you. I had a vision." She kicked her feet and struggled to get free from Avery's grasp.

"Even more reason for you to not be out here alone," Avery shot back as he tightened his grip on her.

"Let me go, Avery!" Zäria pleaded. When he didn't, she tried to send the smallest amount of magic through her hands, just to shock him.

"Ouch!" Avery yelled, letting go of Zäria's arm. "What was that for?"

Zäria stood up and took a step back. "I'm so sorry. I didn't mean to hurt you, but this is something I must do."

Avery stomped his foot in anger as she took flight toward Thordon.

Ambrosia and Goran now had joined forces with the guards,

who protected themselves behind charmed shields as Thordon threw magic at them from the air. Ambrosia and Goran yelled chants and created a protective force field between them and Thordon.

While the others were holding off Thordon, Zäria decided to attack. She used her magic to pull a sword from a guard's hand and sent it toward Thordon's heart as hard as she could. The sword hit him in the chest, but it merely pushed him and then shattered.

I have to think of something else—and quick, Zäria thought. *I'll bet I'm a better flyer than he is.* She flapped her wings hard and flew as fast as she could into a barrel roll, grabbing Thordon's wings as she passed him. She pulled him down, but Thordon fought his wings out of her grip and sent them both tumbling to the ground.

Ambrosia shouted, "Zäria, let go of Thordon, or I'll hit you both!"

Zäria rolled away from him and watched as Ambrosia threw a bolt of magic at Thordon. It only stunned him. "It's not working, Ambrosia!" Zäria yelled back. She was about to throw another blast of magic at him when she saw Eguin stand up behind him. The dragon was several feet taller than any of them. He spread out his glorious velvety purple wings and flexed his claws, exposing his sharp talons. Zäria swallowed hard and took a step back. She noticed the menacing look on Thordon's face.

Rorik cried out to the other guards, "Restrain the dragon!"

Zäria winced as several guards were thrown to the ground when Eguin knocked them down like feathers. Zäria admired the guards' courage as they kept fighting.

Thordon raised up both his hands, and Zäria watched helplessly as he pulled the guards down forcefully and broke the protective barrier Ambrosia had created. He advanced on the guards as they threw all they had at him. Swords, spears, and even shields bounced off the dark faerie. Zäria had to remind herself to breathe when she saw the dragon take to the sky and follow behind Thordon, ready to attack.

Just then, she realized Avery was beside her. He smiled at her at what she felt was the most inappropriate time.

"If you are going to be stubborn, I'm not going to leave your side," he said.

Zäria shook her head. When she looked up, Thordon and Eguin were headed straight for them. She instinctively pushed Avery away, but Thordon was aiming for Avery. She was reminded of her vision. *"No!"* she screamed, as loudly as she could.

She threw as much magic as she had ever tried to pull from her body at Eguin, trying to put some distance between them. It didn't do much, but at least it distracted him enough to slow him down ever so slightly. She flew at Thordon with all her strength as he chased Avery through the air. She crashed into Thordon, sending him into a spin. Avery grabbed hold of Thordon's wings and held him still while Zäria sent another bolt of magic surging into Thordon's chest. She noticed that at the same time, Eguin looked as if he'd taken a blow to the chest as well. She hit Thordon in the leg and watched Eguin suddenly favor his other leg. She realized their connection had become stronger and didn't appear to be wavering.

Ambrosia and Goran came to Zäria's aid. Each took one of her hands and combined their magic against Thordon. While they had Thordon temporarily bound by magic, Zäria said, "Ambrosia, we must break the connection between Thordon and Eguin because it's getting stronger!"

Ambrosia let go of Zäria's hand and flew straight to Rorik.

Zäria and Goran knew they couldn't keep Thordon bound much longer, and Avery lost his grip. Thordon broke free and called Eguin to him. The dragon flapped his wings with so much force that the wind pushed most of the faeries to the ground. Zäria watched in horror as Thordon shot bolt of glowing blue magic from his hands, and Avery's wings stopped flapping as he froze, suspended in midflight. Zäria tried to break Thordon's hold on Avery, but his magic was much too strong. She couldn't tell if Avery was still breathing. Eguin circled above their heads and then swooped down with his jaws wide open. Zäria feared the dragon was going to eat Avery. She screamed out in a panic, "Kill the dragon now!"

Zäria threw all her magic at the dragon to knock him off course; then she pulled another sword from one of the guards and sent it flying. The sword sliced through his right wing. It wasn't enough to ground him, but his jaws missed Avery completely. Zäria saw that it had affected Thordon's ability to fly, causing him to release Avery from his spell. Avery fell to the ground with a thud. Zäria tried to send another attack on Eguin, but Rorik grabbed her arm.

"Why are you attacking my dragon?" he asked.

"Because he was going to kill Avery. He's connected to Thordon. Look at how Thordon's wing was hurt when I cut the dragon's wing. We need to cut the connection."

Thordon screamed, "Eguin, destroy the sanctuary!" The dragon flew over Zäria's head and aimed at the ancient tree. Zäria turned back to Thordon and saw that he was headed for Avery once again.

Ambrosia yelled, "Zäria!" She held up the hilt of a sword to Zäria. "I charmed this one." She tossed the sword in Zäria's direction, and she caught it. Zäria flew at Thordon while she swung the sword over her head with all her might. She sliced straight down, hoping to catch any part of Thordon before he could reach Avery. As if in slow motion, she saw the blade sever both of Thordon's shiny new wings. He crashed to the ground in a bloody heap. Thordon held his prized wings in his hands; tears and blood dripped down his face.

Zäria turned toward the screams behind her. Eguin had fallen when she'd amputated Thordon's wings, and the dragon nearly landed on the guards below. The dragon crashed down and tackled Rorik in the process. Zäria watched as Rorik pulled himself to his feet with a look of horror on his face. She followed his gaze back to the dragon, and saw that Rorik's sword had punctured Eguin's throat. She immediately checked to see if that had affected Thordon, but he was still crying over his wings. The connection evidently was broken between them.

Zäria flew to Avery and landed by his side. He wasn't moving. She rested her head on his chest, but she couldn't tell if his heart was beating. She wanted to scream, but the sound wouldn't come. She tried to use her magic to send a shock through him. She used just enough to make her fingers tingle, but nothing happened. She tried again with a little stronger jolt.

Avery opened his eyes. Zäria started to cry. He was alive. That was the last thing she remembered before she let the exhaustion take over, and she blacked out.

Zäria woke up to Queen Yamani standing over her. She looked around and recognized the room where she had stayed in the sanctuary. She tried to sit up. "Where's Avery?" were the first words out of her mouth.

"Avery is in his chambers. The royal healers are taking care of him. Fynn has been in and out all day with trays of food as well."

Zäria laughed, but it made her whole body hurt. "Ow! Well, it sounds like he's back to normal, then. Can I see him, please?"

"Only if you promise to eat."

"Once I see with my own eyes that Avery is all right, I'll eat anything you want," Zäria said as she tried to get out of her bed.

Yamani grabbed her arm. "Here, let me help you." With Yamani's assistance, Zäria made it to Avery's room across the hall. She opened the door and saw Avery lying in his bed, eating acorn muffins.

"Zäria, you're awake!" Avery exclaimed. He jumped out of bed and ran to Zäria, picked her up, and spun her around. He kissed her on the cheek and said, "I told you that you were my hero." She couldn't help but smile from ear to ear.

Queen Yamani cleared her throat loudly behind them. "I will allow you two time to catch up, eat, and get some rest. When you feel up to it, you are both welcome at the palace in Saizia."

Zäria and Avery both bowed to Yamani and said "Thank you" in unison.

EPILOGUE

Over the course of a year, the kingdom of Saizia was rebuilt. The guards added a stone barrier around the meadow to remind the faeries to never pass into Eerie Hollow again. Zäria moved into the palace and began her training as an heir to the throne. Goran took Veena's place in Saizia. Yamani gave approval to Poppy and Sprout to officially start courting since the pact was abolished.

Avery was knighted and began working with the guards in the palace. Soon after, Zäria and Avery were wed in the palace gardens. Zäria wore her hair up in tendrils entwined with lavender and lilac. Her gown was made from the finest spider silk, which sparkled in the light. Avery was clad in his new guard's uniform made from acorn shells. He complained of the discomfort but swore to Zäria that she was worth it. A year later, they had a faerieling of their own and named her Aväria. They regularly visited King Byron and Queen Xandria in Ellyngshyme.

No one ever saw or heard from Thordon or the remainder of the witch coven, though it was rumored that they might have joined forces.

If that is true, you can believe that the faeries of Saizia will be ready for them.